BUCHANAN GETS MAD

Also by Jonas Ward
in Large Print:

The Name's Buchanan

This Large Print Book carries the
Seal of Approval of N.A.V.H.

BUCHANAN GETS MAD

Jonas Ward

G.K. Hall & Co.
Thorndike, Maine

Published in 1996 by arrangement with Golden West Literary Agency.

G.K. Hall Large Print Western Collection.

The text of this Large Print edition is unabridged.
Other aspects of the book may vary from the original edition.

Set in 16 pt. News Plantin by Minnie B. Raven.

Printed in the United States on permanent paper.

Library of Congress Cataloging in Publication Data

Ward, Jonas, 1939–
    Buchanan gets mad / Jonas Ward.
        p.   cm.
    ISBN 0-7838-1661-8 (lg. print : hc)
    1. Large type books.   I. Title.
[PS3557.A715B83   1996]
813'.54—dc20

95-52455

BUCHANAN GETS MAD

Chapter One

A pebble. A pebble no bigger than a damn pea.

Buchanan suspected that something might be bothering the horse from the moment he got a leg up early that morning. She was half-wild to begin with, Mexican-bred and willful, and his own mind was so determined to make it to Sacramento by nightfall that he kept pushing the little mustang, asking her for more. The job was waiting for him — troubleshooting for the new railroad — but Maguire's letter had reached him so late that now time was a big factor.

So all morning he urged her on. But where she had been so swift and tireless all the long way from the border, now she fought him, kept tossing her head and at last broke stride completely.

A pebble no bigger than a pea, but the filly had pounded it so deep into the hoof of her right foreleg that it made the man sick to think of the agony he'd put her through. Nor was she having any part of his probing for it with a dull-pointed jackknife. It was either shoot her now or get her to a vet. Since he would have shot himself first there wasn't any alternative but to walk her back to the fork in the trail, to the curious signpost he had glanced at in passing.

They reached the spot and he read it again:

BROTHER, THIS IS SALVATION
CALIFORNIA STATE
WE ARE GOD-FEARING
AND LAW-ABIDING
IF YOU ARE NOT,
KEEP OUT OF THIS TOWN
Sidney Hallett, High Sheriff

It had a sour look, that sign, and Buchanan regarded it warily. But where else was there in this vast and lonesome tract if you needed help? There was no place. He led the limping horse up the new trail until it became a street — Genesis Street — and then he noticed something strange about that. For it was coming on noon, the middle of the day, and yet there was not another human being in sight. Nothing stirred, not a speck of dust was raised, and so complete was the stillness that it gave the man an eerie feeling.

Where the hell is everybody? he wondered. Then suddenly that stillness was torn asunder. It was a voice, but what a voice, and it thundered with an awful majesty from the stark-white building that was the church.

It's Sunday, Buchanan realized, grinning as if a joke had been played on him. Three weeks on the open road and a man lost track of each day's identity. It got so he didn't give a damn so long as he had another fifty miles behind him when he hit the blankets at night.

8

Now he had come abreast of the church. So arresting was the voice coming from within that he stopped in the center of the empty street and listened.

". . . AND THE LORD SAID UNTO MOSES — THOU SHALT NOT COMMIT ADULTERY! ANOTHER MAN SHALL NOT KNOW THY NAKEDNESS! ANOTHER MAN SHALL NOT HAVE CARNAL KNOWLEDGE OF THY FLESH . . . !"

The devil's taking his lumps in there, Buchanan thought idly. However, having his own problems to attend to he moved on, unaware of the stupefying effect the preacher's tirade was having on the audience jampacked inside that airless, oven-like church. During the previous forty minutes the tall, gray-faced, black-suited man in the pulpit had spoken to them in generalities, of sin as an abstraction that didn't necessarily apply to those present. There was mention of Sodom and Gomorrah, which he likened to San Francisco and Sacramento. He preached to them in his sonorous tones of wickedness, loose women and Lot's daughters. The general theme of the sermon, if anyone had been able to track it down in all this heat, was the danger to a community — to the town of Salvation — of an immodest woman, an "indecent" woman. Just one, he said. All it took was a single free-and-easy female to send the whole shebang into eternal hellfire.

The usual thing. Generalities. What the congregation more or less expected from stern and unyielding Sidney Hallett. Then, without any warning, he spoke of something they did know about. Birdy's Place — the saloon and gambling house over on River Street. Birdy Warren was the devil's agent, Hallett said. He led good men astray with whisky, took their hard-earned money away with poker tables and roulette wheels. And now this Satan's disciple had added a new temptation. He'd put a young woman to work in his den of iniquity, dressed her in a shameless costume. By this time every head was craning for a look at Ellen Booth, a blonde-haired girl who had been sitting demurely in a side pew near the center. But now, with Hallett's long, accusing arm pointing directly at her, Ellen Booth looked as though someone had driven a fist into her stomach. Her pretty face turned pale, then color rushed into it as mortification overcame her. Still the man in black kept pointing at her and quoting from the Book of Numbers that he knew by heart.

"SINNER, COME FORWARD!" Hallett commanded.

But the girl didn't move — or couldn't move — and she sat there staring up at him in shocked disbelief.

"COME FORWARD!"

Still she didn't budge. Then two husky men came down the aisles, converged on her from either side. They each took an arm, pulled her erect and hustled her to the pulpit. Hallett stepped down, hovered over her menacingly.

"Kneel before me, wanton," he said and the

two men forced her to her knees. Hallett undid the ribbon of her bonnet, took it from her head. Then, using both hands, he unbound the girl's long hair, let it fall in waves that reached nearly to her slim waist.

"Let that be the mark of your sin," he told her sternly. "Let all decent men and women know you for what you are." He raised her up, ungently. "Now go from our sight. You are hereby banished from Salvation!" With that he turned the girl around, started her on the longest walk of her life — the fifty feet to the doors at the rear of the church.

The congregation watched her, some taking the minister's accusation at face value, some wondering if Hallett had any real knowledge of misconduct. The fact was, she did work at Birdy's place — and she did have a husband, Frank, who was away in prison these past three years. Three years is a long, long time. . . .

Buchanan, while this was going on, had reached the end of Genesis Street, where it spilled into Sinai. He now stood looking up and down the main business section of Salvation. Directly opposite was the bank, a squat, adobe building, and stretching out on either side were all the conventional stores that served the community — all of them shuttered now because it was Sunday. But look as he might, Buchanan discovered no veterinary's shingle. Nor a saloon.

What kind of town had he wandered into? he asked himself a little worriedly. Then a voice

11

called to him and he swung to see an old-timer seated in a rocking chair on the porch of a place called Renton's Hotel.

"Who you lookin' for, big fella?" the codger asked.

"The vet, first," Buchanan told him. "Then maybe a dust cutter."

"Find 'em both at Birdy's," the man said, sending a stream of tobacco juice expertly over the porch railing. "But you're too late in the day for Doc Allen," he added. "Got to catch him early, before Birdy opens up."

"Where's Birdy, then?"

"In Damnation," was the unexpected answer, and at Buchanan's quizzical expression the old man cackled. "That's just a name," he explained. "Damnation is what you might call the sportin' section of town, where the trail crews take their fun." He eyed Buchanan appraisingly. "You on the dodge, son," he asked, "or just driftin'?"

"Neither, pop," Buchanan said with patience. "Where's this Damnation located?"

"Go on out Sinai about a quarter mile, then take a right on River Street. You'll know where you are then —" He broke off speaking to stare at the figure of Ellen Booth hurrying toward them from the church. "Now what's that damn scudder done?" the old man demanded, so vehemently that Buchanan glanced to where the old-timer was looking. The girl made a strange sight with her blonde hair all undone, forlorn-looking, and he could read the agitation in her face. When

12

she was close enough the man on the porch spoke again. "What's wrong, Ellen? What's happened to you?" But the girl only shook her head, went past Buchanan without a glance and started up the steps of the rooming house. "I want to help you, Ellie," the old man insisted. "Tell me what's wrong!"

She stopped on the porch, turned to face him.

"He called me an — adultress," she said tonelessly. "I have to leave Salvation."

"Hallett?" the old man cried. "Hallett called you that?"

The girl nodded, biting her lip, and her eyes fell on Buchanan. Formidable, was her first reaction. Violent, crude. And big. Above all he was big. What she was really looking at was a puzzled man of great good-nature, a stranger trying to preserve his neutrality. But she mistook the expression on his battle-scarred face for tough indifference and that crumbled her last defense against the tears welling behind her eyes. She swung away swiftly, averting her face, and dashed inside the building.

"Now what'd you do that for?" the old fellow scolded and Buchanan frowned at him. Plainly, he wanted to get involved no further in the queer goings-on in the town of Salvation.

"So long," he told the man, touching the brim of his battered hat. "Thanks for the information."

The old man watched them from the porch — the limping, restless-looking bronc, the loose-gaited, slope-shouldered giant. *A couple of wild*

13

ones, he decided, wishing that he were walking along with them.

Mild as milk, both of us, Buchanan would have assured him as they covered the prescribed quarter-mile along Sinai Street. Salvation looked not-so-sure of itself down this way. It began to remind him of border towns, and when he had turned into River Street he saw that he had come into a different place altogether. This was a stop along the trail, sure enough, with a gaudy-fronted saloon dominating the surroundings. There was also a down-hearted eating place, a livery, a gunsmith's, a barber's — and if the two-story building trying to hide itself behind tightly closed shutters at the end of the street wasn't a cribhouse then Tom Buchanan was seeing his first one. *Why did they always look so sad?* he wondered again. *Like the last place in the world a man could expect a good time?*

But his business was at Birdy's Place, if the old man's information was right. With a comforting pat on the filly's lean rump he tied her at the rail and went inside. There wasn't much character to Birdy's, merely one sixty-foot room partitioned haphazardly into two. Gambling was on the left. A roulette wheel, keno, birdcage and poker tables. On the right, drinking; at a scarred mahogany bar, with brass rail and ample spittoons, plus a smattering of tables for those who wanted privacy.

Buchanan let the doors swing shut against his back, stood there for a long moment inhaling the

14

fragrance of beer, whisky and tobacco while a home-again grin spread across his face. A half-dozen drinkers were already there, all watching him, and behind the bar a moon-faced, mustachioed bartender whose hand dropped instinctively to the sawed-off shotgun beneath the shelf. Like most, the man felt intimidated by the size of him, the reckless look, the certain knowledge that he didn't come by that scar at his cheekbone from shaving. Now the newcomer was stepping away from the doors, moving toward him, and the bartender noted that the big Colt rode on his hip as if it were part of him.

"What'll it be, friend?" he asked nervously.

"I'm looking for Doc Allen."

"Why?" he said, speaking so sharply that Buchanan leaned toward him in puzzled surprise, took in his features.

"Because my horse is hurting, that's why," he told the man.

"You don't mean him no harm?"

"Hell, no. What's everybody so proddy about?" He straightened up, looked over the others at the bar. "I came into this town for one thing," he said. "A vet. Is he here or isn't he?"

"Doc's in the back room," the bartender told him then. "With Birdy."

Buchanan strode off to the closed door of the private room, knocked on it.

"What do you want?" asked a man's high-pitched voice.

"Got a patient for the vet," Buchanan said and

15

after a moment the door was opened to him by a small man wearing a striped shirt and string tie. His eyes widened at the size of what was filling the doorway and he might have closed it but for Buchanan's restraining arm.

"Don't bring me trouble," the small man said.

Buchanan sighed wearily. "Are you the doc?"

"I'm Birdy Warren. That's Doc Allen." He jerked his thumb to a bearded man slumped on a chair, eyes half-closed. On the table were two empty glasses and a half-gone quart of whisky. "Better come see him tomorrow," Birdy Warren advised.

"Got to see him right now," Buchanan said, moving across the threshold and coming to stand above the drunken veterinary. He put his hand on the shoulder of the man's ragged coat and shook him gently. "I need help, Doc," he told him. "How about it?" Allen grunted, blinked his eyes and reached for the bottle. Buchanan eased it beyond his fingers. "What do you say, Doc?" he asked him again.

"Next week," Allen murmured groggily. "Goin' back to work next week for sure."

"This is a lot of horse," Buchanan insisted. "She needs tending."

"He can't help you," Birdy Warren put in then, his voice sympathetic. "Not today."

"Where does he live?"

"He lives here," the saloonkeeper said, laughing without humor. "Sleeps it off wherever he falls down."

16

"You got a tub?"

"No."

"Where'll I find one?"

"Down to Maude's, most likely. Too early to get into her place, though."

Buchanan bent down, got his shoulder against the vet's midsection and lifted him as another man might handle a child. "I'll have him at the livery in an hour," he said to Birdy. "Be much obliged if somebody would walk my horse down there to meet us."

"Do it myself," Birdy offered, then stood aside as Buchanan walked out of the room with his slack burden.

Chapter Two

When he had finished his rather thoroughgoing job on Ellen Booth, Reverend Hallett gave the deacons the signal to take up the collection — a sizable one — and with that holy services ended. The congregation trooped out, perspiring, exhausted physically and emotionally, and there was Hallett to greet them at the top of the steps. Everyone exchanged some kind of salutation with the man, and even if it was no more than a nod there was deference in it. As many as possible stopped for a personal word, to shake his hand and mouth congratulations for his fine sermon this morning.

Hallett seemed to take their homage as no more than his due as their self-appointed guardian of righteousness. His message to all was that they must remain ever vigilant, that evil must not be given a foothold in Salvation.

Then the last parishioner had gone and the minister made his way back inside the church, to the long table where the deacons were counting out the money. Watching over them was a hard-faced, misshapen hulk of a man whose mouth seemed to be set in a permanent leer. His head and body were formed in gigantic proportions, but the powerful torso rested on legs that were foreshortened, bowed from the uneven weight they supported. He was known to everyone as Bull Hynman, Hallett's right hand.

"What did we take in?" Hallett asked him now in an undertone. "Four hundred?"

Hynman smiled, grotesquely. "That much easy, Sid. Maybe five."

Hallett nodded. "I'll wait for you at the office," he said, taking a flat-crowned black hat from a hook on the wall, setting it squarely on his head and sauntering out into the dazzling sunlight. He walked down the very center of Genesis Street, his figure ramrod straight, and with a certain swinging self-confidence — as if every yard that passed beneath his gleaming black boots belonged to him personally.

At the intersection with Sinai he stopped, almost on the spot where Buchanan had halted fifteen minutes before, and there he stood with an expression of satisfaction etched on his hawklike, coldly handsome face. Then the expression abruptly changed, became disapproving as his glance locked with Pete Nabor's, the arthritic old man in the rocker who had given Buchanan directions. Nabor seemed to bear up under the look directed at him. In fact, there was disapproval of Sidney Hallett in Pete Nabor's lively eyes.

But no word passed between them and now the black-suited man moved on down Sinai until he came to the office he had mentioned to Bull Hynman. SHERIFF it read in gold leaf on the heavily curtained window. Hallett let himself in with a key. It was a sizable room, rectangular in shape, and lying beyond it was the two-cell jail. There was a desk at one end, and a high-backed chair, and atop the desk was a bright, impressive, solid silver star. Beside the star lay a black leather gunbelt with a new pearl-handled Remington .44 jutting from the holster. Hallett picked up the badge, rubbed it affectionately on the lapel of his coat and then pinned it over his heart. He strapped on the gunbelt and that completed the transformation from churchman to lawman.

Along the walls of the office there was a padlocked rifle rack, an assortment of 'wanted' notices from other sheriffs and, directly above the desk, a glass-framed poster whose message had been hand-lettered in 12-point gothic. It read:

THIS IS THE LAW IN SALVATION

1. No One Shall Bear Arms Without A Permit
2. Curfew is Ten P.M.
3. No Female Shall Go Unescorted In Public After Sundown
4. No Alcoholic Beverage Shall Be Consumed Within Town Limits
5. No One Shall Engage In Commerce On the Sabbath
6. No One Shall Be Excused From Church Without A Permit

By order of Sidney Hallett, High Sheriff

Stacked on the floor beside the desk was a box that contained letter-sized reprints of the framed poster, and other copies were displayed prominently in all the stores and each bedroom of the hotel.

Hallett had seated himself behind the desk, awaiting the arrival of Hynman with the money that would go into the safe. Suddenly he cocked his head at a sound outside and got to his feet again. It was the mail stage, enroute to Monterey, and he mentally noted that it was running ahead of schedule. Per instructions, the driver slowed the team to a canter along Sinai Street, angled in to stop directly before the office. A minute later the door to the office opened and the man entered with the mail sack.

"You're early, Bruno," Hallett told him.

"Yeah," Bruno said, emptying the sack on the desktop. He was a man of medium height, with a pockmarked complexion and furtive eyes. Now he leaned across the desk and spoke in a low voice.

"I'm carrying a passenger," he said.

"Is that so?"

"A Mex gal. Nuns put her on board at the mission school. Told me to let her off at Salinas. Seems her old man's bad sick and wants to see her." As he spoke, the stage driver watched Hallett's face closely, looked for some sign of interest. Then he said: "She don't speak English at all," and at this Hallett's eyebrows arched expressively. He took a slender panatela from his

21

vest, bit off the end and lighted it thoughtfully.

"Let's meet your passenger, Bruno," he said, getting up from the desk and following the driver outside. The curtains on the coach were closed and Hallett opened the door. Seated inside the darkened carriage was a black-haired, olive-skinned Mexican girl of nineteen. She looked shy, startled by the abrupt intrusion.

"*Buenos días, señorita,*" Hallett said, his glance traveling upwards from her slim ankles to her firm bosom, resting finally on her pretty, high-cheekboned face. It was bold and unsubtle, and the girl shifted on the seat uncomfortably.

"*¿Por qué nosotros pararemos?*" she asked timidly, not knowing any reason for the coach to halt.

"*Está la ley,*" Hallett told her blandly, "and I carry out the law here." Then, looking up and down the quiet, deserted street he told her in Spanish to come out of the coach.

"No," she answered, shaking her head. Hallett pointed significantly to the gleaming silver star.

"*I* am the law," he said this time. "I command you to come out."

"I am afraid of you," she told him quite frankly. "You wish me harm."

"What's she sayin'?" Bruno the driver asked and Hallett motioned him away impatiently. Suddenly he reached inside the coach, closed his hand over her thin wrist.

"I said — *come out!*" he told her savagely and pulled her to the ground. Quickly, with both hands on her arms, he hurried her inside the

22

office, across to the connecting door and through that to the little jail. The cell door slammed shut and he turned the key in the lock.

Bruno was waiting for him in the office.

"She has some luggage?" Hallett said, breathing heavily from the exertion.

"A trunk and a handbag."

"Scatter them the other side of Hollister," he told him. "I understand some road agents have been working that stretch lately."

"I know what to do."

"Yes," Hallett said. "You're a smart fellow, Bruno. We'll always get along together."

"Yeah, Sheriff. But you know the old saying — fast pay makes fast friends."

"You wouldn't want to have the money on you, would you? Suppose you're searched at Salinas?"

"They won't find nothin' in Salinas," Bruno said. "And I may be taken off this run when I reach Monterey. May not get back this way."

The street door opened and Bull Hynman entered, carrying a large iron box. He and the stage driver exchanged brief nods.

"Give our friend two hundred dollars," Hallett said and Hynman's small black eyes sparked. He opened the box, counted out the money and handed it to Bruno. Then, without inquiring, he opened the connecting door and went on into the jail. Bruno had left when Hynman returned.

"She don't savvy nothin', Sid," the Chief Deputy said.

"Maude will teach her what English she'll need."

"Yeah, I guess," Hynman said, then laughed unpleasantly. "Wouldn't the folks in church be surprised," he said, "if they knew where their money was spent today?"

Hallett, a man devoid of any humor, made no comment. He had been sorting out the mail delivery, in his capacity as Postmaster, holding envelopes up to the light, hefting packages, studying return addresses.

"I kind of go for that little gal myself," Hynman was saying.

"What?" Hallett asked absently. He had suddenly hunched forward, brows knitted, all his attention on a letter gripped tightly in his fingers.

"The one inside," Hynman said. "I wouldn't mind helpin' myself . . ."

Hallett raised his head in agitation. "Take her out to Maude's in the covered wagon," he said sharply.

"Do I got to come right back, Sid?"

"Your lust will be your undoing, Hynman."

"Yeah, but do you need me for anything?"

Hallett waved him away, began ripping open the envelope. It was addressed to *Mrs. Frank Booth, Renton's Hotel, Salvation, California*, and he began reading it without a qualm of conscience.

Dear Ellen:
   I got out of prison this morning. It is a wonderful feeling to be free again and I can't wait until we are together.
   But plans are changed. Instead of coming

24

back there I want you to meet me in San Fran-
cisco. Take a room under the name of Mary
Brown in the Palace Hotel.

I got some business matters to attend to and
will join you there. Leave town without telling
anybody where you are going.

Your husband,
FRANK

Hallett read the letter again, a third time, then replaced it in the envelope. There was deep concern in his face as he took another letter from a desk drawer, an official document from the office of the warden at the penitentiary in Marysville. This was addressed to him, as Sheriff of Salvation, and looked well thumbed as he studied it once more.

Dear Sir:

In reply to your recent inquiry, inmate num-
ber 514, Frank Booth, will be released from
this institution on or about 18 July.

As to his physical condition, Booth appears
to be in excellent health.

The Chief of Guards reports, however, that
during the past year Booth has formed a close
friendship with another inmate, one Luther
Reeves. Reeves is a large man, domineering of
character, and with a well earned reputation
as a desperado. His previous record includes
desertion from the U.S. Army, armed robbery
and rape. He was sentenced to this institution

for a bank holdup for a term of five years. He was released on 3 June, this year.

I include the above information for the reason that the Chief of Guards believes that Booth and Reeves plan to join forces following Booth's release and continue their criminal careers.

Hoping that this supposition is erroneous, I remain

Respectfully yours,
A. HARVEY FLOWERS, WARDEN

Hallett returned the warden's letter to his desk, sat for several minutes deep in thought. Then he left the office, mounted a fine horse tethered out back and rode purposefully out of the town.

It wasn't far, not a long ride, and quite soon he came to a rambling, three-storied white house surrounded by giant oaks that give it a look of peace, security, and impregnable coolness. The sheriff dismounted below the veranda, handed over the reins of his horse to a Mexican boy and climbed the fourteen wooden steps. A gray-haired woman opened the front door, stepped through to greet him.

"Well, I declare!" she said in a pleasant Georgia accent. "What a pleasant surprise! Are you staying with us for dinner, Reverend?" She gave him his ecclesiastical title naturally, without hesitation, as though she thought of him only in that role and not the enforcer of the law.

"Thank you, Sister Martin," Hallett said formally, dampening her own enthusiasm, "but I can't stay. Is your good husband at home?"

Anne Martin laughed, as she did at the slightest provocation. "Now where else would Cyrus be on a Sunday, Reverend?" She held the big door open. "Come on in and I'll call him down." But she didn't have to. Cyrus Martin, short, thick-bodied, nearly bald, was descending the wide, curving staircase, looking at his visitor with an alarmed expression. Very obviously, despite his wife's easy talent for graciousness, the grim-faced man in the wintry black suit was no casual visitor.

"What's wrong, Sidney?" Martin asked, causing Anne to look at him wonderingly.

"A word in private," Hallett said in his abrupt fashion. "You'll excuse us?" he amended to Anne.

"Why, certainly. Has something happened in town?"

"The continuing affairs of men," Hallett told her, telling her nothing.

"We'll go to the study," Martin said, leading the way down the deep carpeted corridor. It was a handsome house, handsomely furnished, but neither more nor less than befitted the president of the Salvation Bank — whose wife had a private income of some three thousand a year. He ushered Sid Hallett inside his study, a comfortable room of leather chairs, pinewood panelling, deep fireplace and shelves lined with the classics and other books well thought of by Victorian standards. Neither man looked quite right in here. Cyrus Martin didn't measure up to the way of life it was supposed to represent. He became suddenly revealed as just a bumbling, ineffectual personality, nervous-eyed, all but faceless. And the room, with its high ceiling, its air of quiet, respectable austerity, only served to bring out the coldness of Sid Hallett, the theatricality of his eccentric dress and mannerisms.

"What's wrong?" the banker asked again.

But the sheriff was engaged in a perusal of the book titles and did not answer immediately. When he did speak it was deceptively casual, with his back still turned to the other man.

"I don't imagine you've forgotten Frank Booth," he said.

"Of course I haven't. What about him?"

"He's paid his debt to society," Hallett said, turning around. "I think he might be coming back to pay us a visit."

Cyrus Martin decided to sit down. The big chair seemed to swallow him whole.

"Have three years passed so quickly?" he said. "I can hardly believe it."

"I imagine the time hasn't been quite so fleeting for young Booth," Hallett remarked drily.

Martin was stroking his mouth, a nervous gesture.

"What will he do — I mean, what will happen when he comes here?"

"He might try to kill us," Hallett said. "He might even try to rob our bank." He spoke as if the two had varying degrees of importance.

"Frank *Booth?*" Martin asked, and apparently there was something incredulous about that.

28

"Oh, he'll be quite changed after three years in Marysville," the sheriff assured him. "And he also has a new friend. A desperado, from the description of him."

"But surely you can do something, Sidney."

"Forewarned is forearmed," Hallett replied. "But the reason I rode out here with the news is primarily to prepare you for any eventuality. This is a time for calm, thoughtful preparation. You and I, Cyrus," the gaunt man said meaningfully, "must stand together in this thing."

"Of course we will, Sidney," Martin said, ruffled by the implication.

"Yes. Of course we will," Hallett echoed. A bleak smile touched his thin lips. "The fellow said it wonderfully in one of your books, Cyrus. We will swim together, or we will sink together." The smile vanished. "Now I think I'll be on my way," he said.

"I'll see you to the door."

"Not necessary," Hallett told him. Then, "We missed you and Mrs. Martin at services this morning."

"I wasn't feeling too well earlier," the banker said.

"We must pay our obligations to Jehovah," Hallett said, and on that sanctimonious note he strode out of the room, out of the house, a resolved man with still another mission to perform on this deceptively quiet Sunday.

Chapter Three

Go 'way from here!" the woman named Maude shrilled unpleasantly from behind the shuttered door. "We don't open till sundown!"

"This ain't trade, ma'am," Buchanan told her, shifting the veterinary to a more comfortable spot on his shoulder. "We just want the use of a tub and some towels."

"What for?"

"To sober up Doc here."

"Why?"

"For an operation."

"He ain't a people's doctor, you damn fool!"

"It's a horse," Buchanan said. "Now come on and open up."

There was another long moment of hesitation, then the bolt was slid back and the door opened. Standing behind it, dressed in a gaudy wrapper, was a cynical-eyed, flabby-cheeked woman of forty-odd years, her dyed hair awry, her face weary beyond description. Buchanan met her tired gaze, smiled tentatively and walked inside before she changed her mind. The door was closed at his back, bolted again, plunging the house into a kind of melancholy darkness.

"You must be crazy with the heat," Maude told him.

30

"I guess. Where's the tub?"

"Upstairs. But don't make any ruckus. My girls are sleeping."

"And some coffee, too. Real hot," Buchanan said, starting up the creaking, rickety flight of stairs, trying to be as quiet as possible under hard conditions.

"Coffee, *too?*" the woman below was crying after him raucously. "Where the hell do you think you are, cowboy?"

"Your girls are sleeping," Buchanan reminded her, making the turn at the top and spying the iron tub in a small room at the end of the hallway. He carried Doc Allen there, stripped him of his clothes and laid him in the tub. Then he went back downstairs, filled two wooden buckets with very cold artesian well water and returned to his patient. The first bucket he threw directly into the vet's bewhiskered face, shocking the man awake, and poured the second one over his midsection. The buckets were systematically re-filled again, unceremoniously emptied. On his third trip to the tub Buchanan found an au- dience of two sleepy-eyed girls, and by this time Doc Allen was wide awake and bawling his in- dignation.

"Don't you come near me!" he shouted at sight of the buckets. "Don't you do it!"

"Sorry, Doc," Buchanan said. "Wish there was some other way," and the cold water went into the tub. The naked man howled anew. Then came the other bucket.

"What're you tryin' to do, kill him?" one of the girls asked.

Buchanan glanced at her, shook his head. "The coffee ought to be ready," he said. "How about bringing it up while I towel him?"

"What do you take me for," she said tartly, "your maid?"

Now he looked her over, from head to toe, his eyes twinkling. "No," he said, "I guess I don't take you for my maid."

"I'll get the coffee, honey," the other one said and went off down the corridor with much hip-swinging. When she got back Buchanan had the still-furious veterinary dry and partly dressed again.

"Much obliged," he said to the girl, taking the steaming mug from her hands.

"You're real polite," she told him, her voice guileless. "You look awful fierce, but I just bet you're gentle."

"As a lamb," Buchanan agreed with a grin, then turned to Allen. "Here you go, Doc," he said, "Drink this down and you'll be ready to do business."

"Who in the name of hell are you, anyhow?" Allen demanded. "What's goin' on around here today?"

"Down the hatch," Buchanan coaxed, holding the coffee to the other man's lips. "You got a sick horse waiting for you." He and Allen looked into each other's eyes for a moment, then the vet took the mug in his own hands and began drinking it.

"Damnedest outrage I ever heard of," he complained between swallows. "Man don't have any rights at all these days." He went on in that vein until the coffee was gone; then Buchanan helped him to his feet and they started out of the dreary place.

They were halfway down the stairs when someone began pounding heavily on the door. Maude rushed out to peer through the shutter, but this time she opened it without protest. Bull Hynman came inside, roughly shoving the sobbing, disheveled Mexican girl before him.

"Brought you a new one, Maude," Hynman said, a hard, arrogant smile on his face. Buchanan regarded him from the staircase in some surprise, never having seen a procurer before with a Chief Deputy's star on his fancy silk shirt. He wondered, too, about the new recruit.

"*¡No lo quiero!*" she was pleading. "*¡Déjeme de ir!*"

"What's she saying, anyhow?" Hynman asked querulously.

"She says to let her go," Buchanan answered him quietly, moving to the bottom of the stairs with the vet. "She says she don't want to be in here."

"That's too bad," Hynman said. "Step aside, bucko, I'm going upstairs."

"But she don't want to."

Hynman glowered at him, dumbfounded for an instant. "What the hell is it to you?" he growled dangerously.

Buchanan was looking down into the girl's terrified face, glancing at the hard grip the man had on her bare shoulders.

"Turn the lady loose, mister," he said. Hynman's right hand fell away, snaked the gun free of its holster. He jammed it into Buchanan's flat stomach.

"Get outta here," he said, and Buchanan felt the doctor beside him stiffen with fear, start to sway perilously. The cold water-and-coffee treatment wasn't going to sustain him much longer.

"Take that shooter out of my belly," he told Bull Hynman. "I got other business."

"Damn well told you have," Hynman said, pulling the gun back but holding it in his fist. "Beat it."

Buchanan walked Allen on out of the bordello, took him to the livery stable where Birdy Warren was waiting as promised with the hurting mustang. The man looked to be hard put upon.

"Godamighty!" he complained. "This critter don't mind at all. Meanest animal I ever been near."

"She gets notions sometimes," Buchanan admitted. "But she sure can run."

"I'll bet she can," Doc Allen said admiringly, a new sound in his voice as he approached the wall-eyed horse unhesitatingly. "What's wrong, girl?" he asked, stroking her cheek and lower jaw with the flat of his hand. "Hurt to stand on that hoof, does it?" And whatever it was about the man, the horse responded immediately, relaxed and grew docile before their eyes.

"She'd've bitten me twice by now," Birdy said. "And kicked me to boot."

The vet bent down, still talking soothingly, took the filly's pastern and fetlock between his cupped hands and lifted the injured hoof for an examination. "Well, no wonder," he said. "Can't run much with that stone in there, can you, girl?"

"Serious, Doc?" Buchanan asked.

"Would've been," Allen said. "By tonight. Glad you took strong measures like you did," he added drily, looking Buchanan squarely in the face. "All right, let's get her into the rig. About time she had some comfort." What he spoke of as 'the rig' was a special harness, homemade-looking and suspended between the sides of the end stall. Attached to the top of the harness was a thick rope which ran through a pulley in an overhead cross-beam, then across to a second pulley nailed to the side of the stable. Buchanan helped guide his horse into the harness, tightened the cinches on the extra-thick breast collar, bellyband and breeching. The vet himself put on the restraining knee irons that would discourage any leg thrashing.

"Haul away," he said then and Buchanan pulled on the free end of the rope, raising the horse a good five feet off the ground with surprisingly little effort. "High enough," Allen told him and he snugged the rope fast to a cleat.

"Need me for anything else?"

"Nope. Where you going?"

"For a walk."

Allen laughed at him. "Don't tell me a big galoot like you owns a queasy stomach?"

"Could be, Doc."

"Well, come back in half an hour," Allen said. "And when you do, have a bottle in your hand. I got to get caught up on my schedule again."

"Will do," Buchanan said and left the stable with Birdy. It had been dark and cool in there; it was bright and hot outside. He pulled his hat brim down low to shield his eyes from the glare.

"You sure handled Doc good," Birdy said admiringly. "He can be an ornery customer when his snoot's full."

"Quite a way with a horse," Buchanan commented. Their steps had carried them to the saloon entrance and Birdy started in, then stopped in surprise.

"Ain't you comin' inside, mister? Stand you a drink."

"In a while, Birdy. Got a date down the street."

Birdy Warren leered at him, man-to-man fashion. "In the middle of the day?" he asked him. "You must be some primed."

"Some," Buchanan agreed, walking off alone in the direction of the bordello, indifferent in his own mind as to what the saloonkeeper thought he was about. His long-legged stride was measured but unhurried, his arms swung easily at his side, and only when he was standing before the door of the place again, when he squared his broad shoulders for the briefest instant, did he seem to be anything else but a puncher out on the town. He knocked three times on the door.

"Now what do you want?"

"I came back for the little lady," Buchanan said without raising his voice. "Open up."

"Get away, y'hear? Get out! I spotted you for a trouble maker from the start."

"Open the door."

"Bull!" she cried then. "Come down here! Take care of this saddle bum outside!"

"What the hell does he want?"

"Trouble!" she bawled and Buchanan could hear the man inside the place laugh.

"Trouble he'll get," Hynman promised. "Let him in."

"And get myself killed? I will not!"

So be it, Buchanan decided, hitting the door hard with knee and shoulder. He felt it sag in its frame, heard the wood around the metal bolt splinter.

"Come and get it, bucko!" Bull Hynman roared from the other side and Buchanan had a picture of the man standing atop the stairs, gun drawn. Buchanan stepped back, raised his booted foot and launched a powerful kick at the door. It sprung open, and he threw himself aside as three booming shots came winging down from above. Buchanan triggered two covering bursts of his own into their echo, charged low through the doorway and kept going until he had the semi-protection of the stairwell itself.

"Get him, Bull! Get him!" Maude screamed from the safety of the parlor and there followed a moment of tense quiet. Buchanan waited, listening, and then he heard the man above him begin to make a furtive movement to gain the landing directly overhead. He matched steps with him, kept edging forward.

They stood revealed to each other in the same instant, fired together. Buchanan's snap shot blew the man's gun right out of his hand, sent him reeling back against the wall. Buchanan himself was spun halfway around by a slug that seared his rib cage, but he kept his balance, gained the stairs and mounted them a pair at a time.

"Pick yourself up, Deputy," he told the dazed Hynman, seeing no wound, marveling at the fellow's luck that he wasn't dying on the floor. He retrieved the fallen gun, examined the bullet-smashed cylinder and hammer in disbelief, wondered what the odds would be against such a thing happening.

"Now what?" Hynman asked, his voice sullen but unafraid.

"Here's a souvenir for you," Buchanan said, tossing the busted .45 to him. "Keep it around to remind you you're on borrowed time."

Hynman took both the gun and the advice in bad grace, didn't seem impressed at all with his narrow brush. The gaze he leveled at Buchanan was truculent, still-threatening. Buchanan shrugged, turned his back to him and started down the second floor corridor. First one door opened, then a second, and the two girls he had seen before put their frightened heads out. A third door stayed closed and Buchanan opened it himself.

The terror-stricken Mexican girl cowered in the furthest corner of the shabby little room. It was plain in her eyes that she expected no better from him than she'd gotten from the other man.

"It's all right now," Buchanan said gently but she only stared at him, arms crisscrossed in front of her body in pathetic defense. "*¿No habla inglés?*" Buchanan asked her then and she shook her head slowly. "*No tiene miedo,*" he said, his voice reassuring. "I won't hurt you. I'm taking you out of here."

She heard and wanted to believe — but there was such a wildness to him.

"Are you," she asked, "a man of honor?"

"I mean you no harm, señorita."

She took a step toward him, another, then stopped abruptly. "You are hurt," she told him. "You are bleeding."

"I know," he said. "That's why we ought to get out of here now."

She nodded, came all the way out of the room and Buchanan escorted her back dawn the hallway. Waiting for them at the top of the landing, barring their way like a mastiff, was Bull Hynman. The girl saw him, faltered, and Buchanan moved out in front of her. When they were some thirty feet from Hynman he spoke to him.

"We're coming through," he said. "Stand aside."

"Not her," Hynman said. "She's bought and paid for." In his hand was the gun, held by the long barrel.

"Coming through," Buchanan told him again.

"You don't know what you're buckin' here!" Hynman snarled. He swung the gun at Buchanan's head, club-fashion, and Buchanan seemed to be stepping right into its murderous path. But all at once the big man's torso swerved, right to left, taking Hynman's blow on his enormous shoulder, then swerved back again and Hynman was lifted clear of the floor by the fist that exploded against his chin. That finished Hallett's deputy and Buchanan guided the girl around his sprawled, unconscious figure, took her down the flight of stairs. Maude awaited them there, her harridan's face venomous.

"You'll be back!" she shrilled, pointing a finger at the girl, then turned her eyes up to Buchanan. "And they'll get you," she told him. "They'll get you good."

"*¿Qué ella dice?*" the girl asked Buchanan worriedly.

"*Nada,*" he said, moving her on out the door.

"Tell her!" Maude yelled at their backs. "Tell her she'll be back in here tonight. And you'll be dead!"

"*¡Qué los malos!*" the girl said.

"Forget them," Buchanan said, but he was thinking himself of this Sidney Hallett, the so-

40

called High Sheriff who preached the wrath of God and helped stock a crib-house, all in one day. It took all kinds to fill up a world, he supposed, and then had his musings interrupted. The gunplay, brief but startling, had lured the barflies out into the street. They stood clustered in front of the saloon, blinking like so many owls in the unaccustomed sunlight as they marked the progress of the man and his companion.

"What in hell you been up to now?" Birdy Warren asked, his voice strung with excitement and a measure of concern. "What happened down there?"

"By damn," cried another, "the drifter's raided the *lupanar!* Plucked one of Maude's chippies right outta the coop!"

Buchanan caught that one's eye. "She ain't a chippie," he told him flatly, "and she wasn't volunteering for the work." Then his glance roved the group of faces. "Anybody here the barber?" he asked.

"That's me."

"I need a bandage, friend. Can you fix me up?"

"You bet."

"Godamighty, you *are* hit," Birdy chirped. "Come on upstairs and get off your feet. Fred," he said to the barber, "bring your stuff back here." He had Buchanan by the arm, began leading him inside. Suddenly the big man stopped in his tracks, swung around. The girl was still standing there, forlorn-looking.

41

"What are you going to do?" he asked in her own language.

She shook her head. "I do not know, señor."

"Where are your people?"

"My father is in Salinas."

"*Salinas?*" he echoed, frowning, thinking that she was a hell of a way from home. "How are you going to get to Salinas?"

"I do not know," she said again.

The frown deepened into a scowl. Sacramento was that way, Salinas the other. He looked down at Birdy.

"Anybody going to Salinas?" he asked him.

"Next stage through here is Wednesday," he said.

Buchanan rubbed at the stubble on his chin, sighed unhappily. "You better stay with me for now," he told the girl. "We'll figure out something."

She smiled for the first time, came forward without hesitation. "Yes," she said, "I will stay with you."

Birdy Warren spoke to him then in an undertone. "I don't savvy the lingo between you and her," he said, "but you better watch yourself."

There was a sudden racket down the street and everyone turned to see a fast-driven covered wagon hurtling away from the bordello. High on the seat was Bull Hynman, his face bruised and furious, and as the wagon raced by he raised his fist to Buchanan.

"I'll be back, you sonofabitch!" he roared. "I'll be back!"

They watched him move on, raising a cloud of dust behind him, then swing right at the end of River Street and disappear.

"I guess you *better* watch yourself," Birdy Warren said to Buchanan. "What'd you want to tangle with that rat for?"

"Mister," he answered, "I don't want to tangle with anybody ever. Leave it to me and I'd be halfway to Sacramento."

"What'll you do up there?"

"Work," Buchanan said. "The Central Pacific is getting ready to lay tracks."

The other man nodded his head. "That's work with a future in it," he said. "You're more than I figured you for."

Chapter Four

From the single window in her little room on the top floor of the hotel, Ellen Booth looked down on Salvation and tried to see it as another person might, a total stranger. Such a quiet little town, so neat and peaceful — a wonderful place to settle in, to get married and raise a family. Nothing unpleasant could ever happen in law-abiding, God-worshiping Salvation.

Her glance took in the bank building, and the game she was trying to play abruptly ended. For it was there she had first seen Frank Booth, the new teller that Mr. Martin had hired. It was a Saturday morning and she'd come down from the ranch with her father. It was only because he was so ill that she'd gone into the bank with him while he made another payment on the loan. Mr. Martin was in conference with Sheriff Hallett, but the transaction was a routine one and Mr. Booth could handle it.

He was courteous and businesslike, spoke knowledgeably to her father of ranching. In answer to his questions he'd explained that he was from San Francisco, that he'd come down here with the hope of acquiring some cattle land himself. Ellen was sitting off to one side, noticing that he was of medium height, slim, that he dressed and talked quite differently from the other young men of the region, and that he was quite good-looking when he smiled. He was even more good-looking when her ever-curious father asked if he were married and he said no, not yet. Ellen didn't think he'd even noticed her until, just as they were leaving, he asked permission to call at the ranch the next evening. Her father had looked to her, she'd nodded, and that was how the courtship began.

Booth became a regular visitor for Sunday supper after that, took her to the rare dances that Sheriff Hallett permitted — July the Fourth, New Year's Eve, Drover's Day — and when it was announced that Ellen Henry was marrying Frank Booth no one in Salvation was surprised. Excepting, of all people, Sidney Hallett, and his reaction to the betrothal disturbed the bride-to-be considerably. He made a special trip to the ranch in that fine black buggy of his, but whether he was there as minister or sheriff neither she nor her father could figure out.

But he was very angry when he spoke to old Tom Henry and his voice carried throughout the small house.

"What do you know, Brother Henry, of this city slicker?" Hallett demanded. "What kind of life has he led in that den of iniquity, San Francisco?"

And her father had answered that the bank must have checked his references, looked into his past, and pointed out that Hallett, himself, was

45

a director of the bank and a major stockholder.

"I'm talking of this stranger's morals, not his business credentials!" Hallett said very harshly. "How do you know he hasn't left a wife and family in San Francisco?"

"Has he?" Tom Henry asked.

"You're the girl's father. That's for you to find out! It's your duty, Brother!"

Ellen's father said then that he thought Hallett was searching for trouble where none existed, that he was satisfied with Frank Booth as a son-in-law.

"Well, I am not," the sheriff told him. "My advice to you is to postpone this marriage, to keep Booth away from your daughter until you've searched his background."

That was when Ellen had come out of her room and walked into the parlor. Just a single lamp burned in there, and the shadow of Hallett's tall, craggy figure seemed ominous and overpowering to the seventeen-year-old girl. But she found the courage to speak to him.

"What do you know of Frank Booth?"

"That he comes from a sinful place," Hallett said. "That you would do better to marry someone you have known nearly all your life."

"But I'm not in love with anyone like that."

"Love?" he'd said, the word an abomination on his lips. "Love? What can you know of love?"

"Only that I love Frank Booth," she answered simply and that seemed to feed fuel to his wrath.

"Physical love!" he shouted down at her. "Carnal love! That is what you feel for this simpering,

46

grinning fool with his citified ways! He has se-
duced you —"

Her father had intervened then, considerably
wrought-up himself, and in the sharp exchange
between them Tom Henry had ordered Hallett
from his home. Hallett had stormed out, but not
without threats and a vague warning that they
would both regret it if Ellen married Booth. And
hardly was he gone but Tom Henry had another
seizure, a serious one that took his life three short
days later. So the young girl had a funeral before
a wedding. Though her father's health had been
quite frail she could not help but feel that Sid
Hallett's night visit had considerably shortened
his life. She also had time to think of the things
he said that night, especially about marrying
someone she had known all her life. Among those
would have been Hallett himself — a man more
than twice her own age.

She told herself that it was impossible he could
have meant that. However the thought kept re-
curring, grew worrisome when Hallett took an
active, personal interest in settling her father's
meager estate. Banker Martin was named executor
in the will, but it was the sheriff who handled
the details. The ranch had been left to her, along
with a small amount of cash, but there was still
some three thousand dollars owing the bank for
which the land was collateral. It was on this matter
that Hallett really perplexed the girl — when
he offered to pay off the loan himself and suggested that she should have the help and com-

panionship of a mature, experienced man in the management of the ranch.

"Frank will run the place when we are married," she told him. Hallett's voice had been pleasant up until then. Now it was cold.

"You are not going to marry Booth," he told her flatly. "I forbid it."

"*You* forbid it?"

"Your father is gone, girl. You need someone else to guide you."

"But my father approved of Frank. You know that."

"I know that your father was a very sick man. He did not have full possession of his faculties."

"He did!"

Hallett shook his head. "Booth took advantage of both of you. He doesn't deserve to have such a prize as yourself, Ellen."

She broke off the conversation, got away from him almost in terror, and at her insistence she and Frank married within a week. The young man assumed all responsibilities for the money owed on the property, but convinced his bride that it would be better if he continued working at the bank for at least another year. The cattle market, he told her, was uncertain — but his weekly salary from Cyrus Martin was money they could count on.

They were married six short months when it happened, when that leering deputy, Hynman, rode out to the ranch to tell her that Frank was under arrest. Embezzlement. A shortage in

Frank's accounts of five thousand dollars. And as if his information wasn't cataclysmic enough, Bull Hynman added a personal touch that made his visit a complete nightmare.

Ellen had run to the bedroom, to change from the workdress into something better, and though she had closed the door she had not considered it necessary to lock it. The hulking, beady-eyed Hynman came into the room and found her in only a thin cotton undergarment. She ordered him out and he shook his head.

"I've been waitin' for this a long time," he said.

"Get out!" she told him again. "I've got to get dressed. I've got to go to my husband."

"You can't help him," Hynman said. "The case is open and shut."

"Frank didn't steal anything!"

"He stole five thousand dollars. And he'll be in prison a long time. Lady, you need all the friends you can get right now."

"I don't need you!" she screamed at him. He lunged for her, broke the strap of the undergarment, tried to force her down on the bed. But Ellen squirmed out of his grip, made her way out to the room her father had used for an office. Still in the desk was his old single-shot Remington — and when she levelled it at Hynman's chest neither of them knew whether it was loaded. Hynman, however, decided to bide his time, figured that she would be available to him in this lonely old house another night.

He left and Ellen rode into Salvation. Frank's face was haggard, his eyes sunken as he fell to his knees in the cell and swore his innocence. Ellen believed her husband, out of her love for him, but so damning was the evidence at his trial that even her faith was shaken. The most telling witness against Frank Booth was a man named Poindexter, a U.S. Marshal from San Francisco. Poindexter read to the jury an affidavit taken from a woman identified as Ruby Fowler. Ruby Fowler had taken her own life, and on her death-bed confessed to receiving five thousand dollars from Frank Booth — and, in turn, giving the money to a lover who had run out on her.

Frank denied Poindexter's testimony, swore he'd never laid eyes on Ruby Fowler. Then he was shown a ring, one which Ellen from her seat in the jammed courtroom identified as Frank's own signet. Frank also admitted ownership, claimed that he had lost it in the bank's washroom months before. The marshal was then recalled to the stand.

"Have you ever seen this ring, Mr. Poindexter?"

"I have. I brought it down here myself from San Francisco."

"And how did you come to have it?"

Poindexter looked at Frank Booth, then to the jury. "I found that ring," he said, "among the effects of the late Ruby Fowler."

The jury voted right in the box — guilty — and Sidney Hallett, as magistrate, sentenced him to prison for twenty years. That was stern justice, and Ellen persuaded Frank's lawyer to appeal to the state court. The conviction was upheld, but the sentence was reduced to a minimum of three years and a maximum of ten.

Hallett allowed Ellen to see Frank only one more time, in the cell again, and once more Booth pleaded his innocence to her. But her doubts now came between them like a wall.

"I'd still love you, Frank," she told him. "No matter what mistake you made."

"I didn't do it, Ellen," he insisted.

"But you're going away," she said tearfully. "Don't you want to tell me everything about you and Ruby Fowler?"

Booth shook his head stubbornly, said there was nothing to tell about Ruby Fowler. Ellen kissed him and Bull Hynman, of all undesirable people, came to take Booth to the waiting stage.

Two nights later, after midnight, Hynman visited her at the ranch, tried to force himself inside. But now Ellen was armed with a shotgun and the deputy left with his tail between his legs. Next morning, Ellen moved into this room at the hotel, eked out a haphazard living as a waitress in the dining room, a salesgirl at the mercantile and even did menial labor from time to time. The town was completely dependent on the cattle market, and Ellen's employment and joblessness fluctuated with the price of cows at the slaughterhouse.

A year ago Birdy Warren had offered her a

job in his place — scandalizing the young girl to some degree — and whenever he might see her the saloonkeeper repeated the offer. And last month, when she lost her last job in Mrs. Meeker's dress shop, Ellen went to work in Birdy's.

Sid Hallett had pressed his suit all this time. But never publicly, never really saying outright what he expected her to do about him. He did suggest that she should divorce Frank Booth, promised that Booth would remain in prison for the full term of ten years. Her answer was always the same — a firm "No." But Hallett never was clear about what his intentions would be if the answer had been the one he wanted. He pressed his attentions furtively and kept close watch on her activities — so close that Bull Hynman was kept from making any advances of his own. Hynman didn't guess that his boss had a personal interest in Ellen Booth. He thought that it had some vague connection with the embezzlement of the bank by her husband, that there might be other monies involved and she knew of them.

And then this Sunday morning, like a bolt from the blue, Hallett had turned on her from the pulpit, accused her without any cause of adultery, made her job at Birdy's seem shameful, and banished her from the town. Where was she supposed to go? What was she supposed to do? Her only reason for staying in Salvation — of bearing the onus of a thief's wife — was to be here when her husband returned, to pick up the threads of their brief life together and start anew. They could go to the ranch, she thought, where there would be no people to bother them and plenty of hard work to make them forget what had happened in the past. But even that was not to be now — thanks to Sid Hallett.

Such a quiet little town, a wonderful place to settle and marry and raise a family. As Ellen Booth relived these last four years her glance moved from the bank's façade to the disappearing figure of the big cowpoke leading the limping horse down Sinai Street toward Damnation. That was the life, she thought in self-compassion. No worries, no problems; just come as you please, go as you please, do as you please. She saw his face again, very clearly, and once again passed judgment on him as tough and distant, unapproachable.

Ellen was still at the window when Sidney Hallett came into view, stopped for a long moment and then moved on toward his office. She turned away, reminded of his injunction, packed her few belongings in a cardboard suitcase and left the hotel to walk herself in the direction of River Street. For some reason that the girl couldn't explain she felt that she would be among her own kind of people there, that men like Birdy Warren and poor old Doc Allen could advise her what to do. For Hallett was against them, too. Had vowed publicly to drive them out.

But neither of them was there when she arrived at the saloon. According to the barkeep, Sam, Allen had left on the shoulder of a big stranger.

Birdy had gone out a bit later, taken the stranger's horse to the livery. And so far as Sam could make out from eavesdropping, it had something to do with a little stone the horse had picked up in her hoof. None of it made much sense to Ellen and she climbed the flight of steps to her dressing room on the floor above. But she didn't change into one of the three sequined, short-skirted and tight-bodiced gowns Birdy had bought for her to work in. Instead she waited, not sure what her status was, and presently there was a knock on the door. It was Birdy.

"I'm in trouble," Ellen told him.

"I heard what happened in church, Ellie. I'm awful sorry."

"Sorry? What fault is it of yours?"

"I'm not blind," he said. "Not like those sheep uptown that Sid Hallett keeps all flocked and ignorant. Hallett's after you, kid," he told her. "He watches over you like a hawk on a sparrow. I knew that when I first offered you a job here. Figured he'd give up if you went over to my side of the street." The small man shook his head ruefully. "I figured wrong," he said. "Looks like if he can't have you, nobody can."

It was calmly spoken, as matter-of-factly as Birdy could speak in his high-pitched voice, but the girl was appalled to hear someone else put her own dark fears into words.

"If he can't," she asked him, "nobody can?"

"You're talking about your husband," Birdy said. "I don't know anything about that. I wasn't

54

even at his trial."

"A government marshal gave evidence," she said. "It must have been true."

"They ain't angels, honey, take it from me. You get west of Chicago and you see some damn strange things . . ."

The gunfire down at Maude's broke into his conversation, sent him to the shade-drawn window. He raised the shade, leaned out over the sill just a moment too late to see Buchanan's unorthodox entrance into the bawdyhouse.

"What is it?" Ellen asked.

"Damned if I know," Birdy said. "But that wild scudder just took off for Maude's."

"Who?"

"Fella with a hurt horse. Hauled Doc Allen over there to sober him up." Birdy laughed. "Guess he took a shine to one of Maude's girls."

Again there were gunshots coming from within the house at the end of the street.

"Man, man," Birdy said reprovingly. "Didn't figure him to be so proddy."

"He looked like a roughneck to me," Ellen said. "Where are you going?"

"Downstairs," Birdy answered, opening the door. "Find out what's going on."

The saloonkeeper left her, and when Buchanan made his surprising exit from Maude's, Ellen was a silent observer from the upstairs window. The next thing she knew, Birdy was leading the wounded man inside and she heard their footsteps ascending the stairs to the dressing room.

"Can we come in, Ellie?" Birdy asked. She opened the door, stood aside while they entered. If the dressing room had been small before it shrunk considerably the moment Buchanan crossed the threshold.

"This is Ellen Booth," Birdy said. "Don't think I ever heard your name."

"Tom Buchanan. Pleased to meet you." He swept off his hat and Ellen nodded to him, wondering what in the world he found to smile about with his shirt all soaked in blood and Bull Hynman threatening even more damage.

"Stretch out on that couch there," Birdy told him. "Let's get that shirt off your back and have a looksee."

"That's no treat for the ladies," Buchanan said and then spoke to the Mexican. "*Sale usted, por favor.*"

"I would rather stay," she answered. "I can do something to help, perhaps."

"But this won't be agreeable . . ."

"Instead of arguing about it," Ellen said, "why don't you just take your shirt off?"

Buchanan blinked at her in surprise, began to do as she told him to. The barber made his way inside then, carrying towels, bandage and a pan of water. He set to work quickly, almost professionally, and his comment when the four-inch-long wound was exposed was an expressive whistle.

"I bruise easy," Buchanan said, sounding almost apologetic.

"And you'd have died easy, buster, if that slug had come another inch inside." He began wrapping the gauze around Buchanan's ribs.

"Where'd you get that one?" Birdy Warren asked, pointing to a bullet scar high on his chest. Buchanan rubbed his finger along the old wound, his face thoughtful.

"Picked it up a year ago," he said. "Compliments of a friend."

"Got another one on your arm there," Birdy said. "And by golly look at this beauty." He turned to Ellen. "Ever seen the likes of it?"

"No," she said, "I didn't. But I imagine Mr. Buchanan earned them."

"And paid back with interest, hey, Tom?" Birdy said admiringly.

"You about through?" Buchanan asked the barber.

"Through as I'll ever be."

"What's the bill?"

"A dollar?" the man said questioningly.

"Fair enough," Buchanan told him, reaching into his trousers for a cartwheel. But when he started to pull on the grisly-looking shirt again, Ellen Booth spoke up.

"Don't you have anything else to wear?"

"My butler's gone on ahead with all the trunks," he answered drily.

"Wait a minute," Birdy said. "I'll get you something. May not fit, but it'll be clean." He left the room and so did the barber, leaving Buchanan to stand half-dressed and uncomfortable

57

between the two females.

"*¿Es su mujer?*" the Mexican one asked him and he shook his head.

"What did she say?" Ellen asked.

"She asked me if you're my woman."

"What ever gave her an idea like that?"

"Don't ask me."

"Tell her that I'm married," Ellen said.

"Why?"

"I just want her to know."

Buchanan shrugged. "*La señora es casada,*" he said obediently to the dark-haired girl.

"*Yo estoy feliz,*" she said, smiling at Ellen.

"She says she's happy," Buchanan translated.

"Tell her thank you."

"*La señora dice gracias,*" Buchanan said.

"*De nada.*"

"You're welcome," Buchanan told Ellen.

"What's her name?"

"I don't know."

"You had a gunfight over her and you don't know her name?"

"It wasn't exactly a fight *over* her."

"Then what was it?"

"Well — a difference of opinion. What I mean is, there was nothing personal."

Ellen looked at him curiously. "Ask her her name," she said.

Buchanan sighed, turned to the Mexican. "*¿Cómo se llama Ud?*"

"*Yo se llamo Juanita María Isabel Henriquez y del Vayez,*" the girl answered brightly.

"Juanita," Buchanan told Ellen.

"Tell her my name is Ellen Booth."

"*La señora se llama Elena,*" he reported dutifully.

"*Ella es muy linda,*" Juanita said.

"*Sí.*"

"What was that?" Ellen asked.

"Juanita thinks you're good-looking," he explained and the blonde girl colored.

"I think she is very pretty," she said.

"*La señora dice usted es muy linda también,*" he told the other one. Then the door opened, Birdy came in with a gray denim shirt, and Buchanan looked like a man reprieved. He put his arms through the shirt, buttoned it snugly across his chest.

"Biggest one Perley had in stock," Birdy said.

"How much?" Buchanan asked, reaching into his pocket.

"On the house," the saloonkeeper said. "Can I have the old one, for a souvenir? Want to hang it over the bar mirror."

"You serious?"

"Damn right I am. And now I'm going to take you downstairs and buy you a drink."

Buchanan looked suddenly stricken. "The Doc," he said unhappily. "Promised to bring him a bottle."

"All took care of. And that mean-eyed bronc of yours is took care of, too."

"Wonder can I ride on out of here?"

"What's the big hurry?"

"The job I mentioned."

"Hell, they'll be years building that railroad. Come on down and have a drink with the boys." He turned to Ellen. "You two pretty gals come along, too. Brighten up the place."

The four of them, making an odd assortment, left together.

Chapter Five

When Sid Hallett returned from his visit to Cyrus Martin's house he dismounted before the hotel and strode inside.

"Can I help you, Sheriff?" the desk clerk asked, made nervous just by the man's appearance in the place.

Hallett shook his head. "I'm going up to see Mrs. Booth," he said.

"She's checked out," the clerk informed him.

"When?"

"A little after noon."

"Carrying any luggage?"

"Yes, sir, a traveling bag."

"Which way was she headed?"

"She turned up that way," he said, pointing toward River Street, and the sheriff promptly left him, returned to his office. There were three men taking their leisure in there — special deputies at the moment, but who doubled as deacons of the church, collection takers and whatever else Hallett needed them for. They all climbed to their feet, seemed to appear apologetic for their inactivity on this peaceful Sunday. Hallett went by them to his desk, opened a drawer and took out a legal document. It was an arrest warrant, already signed by 'Sidney Hallett, Magistrate,' directing

'Sidney Hallett, Sheriff, and/or his Deputy' to take into lawful custody (blank) for the charge of (blank). Into these blank spaces he now wrote 'Mrs. Frank Booth' and 'Accessory before the crime.'

"Come here, Lafe," Hallett said then and the block-shouldered, surly-faced deputy came forward. "Take the buggy and serve this warrant on Mrs. Booth. You'll most likely find her on River Street, in the saloon. If you have any trouble —" He broke off, looked beyond Lafe to another deputy. "You ride along with him, Enos. Don't let Birdy Warren or anyone else interfere with you. I want that woman brought back here within the hour."

They left, neither man bothering to glance at the warrant. If they had been told to hang Ellen Booth by the neck they would have ridden off with the same stolid, impassive resolve. There was, however, an interruption. Bull Hynman met them coming the other way along Sinai Street.

"Where the hell do you think you're goin'?" he demanded angrily.

"Birdy's place," Lafe grunted. "Who hit ya?"

"*Birdy's?* Why?"

"Boss wants Mrs. Booth brought in. Who hit ya?"

"What's he want with her?"

"Don't know. Who — ?"

"None of yer friggin' business. Get back here quick. I got work for you, too."

They parted, and after a minute's more riding

Enos spoke to his partner. "Things sure picked up all of a sudden."

"Yeh. Who you figured hit the bull?"

"Don't know," Enos said. "Wished I'd've seen it, though. Jesus, I hate that pushy bastard."

He and Lafe exchanged a glance, traveled the rest of the way to Birdy's place in silence. As they dismounted they seemed to carry themselves differently, more truculently, as if their mission here was a matter of grave importance. In that mood they threw open the swinging doors of Birdy's saloon and entered.

"Oh, oh!" Birdy said. "Trouble."

Buchanan, standing at the bar, looked up into the mirror, saw the hulking pair, noted the badges on their shirtfronts.

"Now take it easy, Tom," Birdy said, speaking behind his hand. "They're a couple of bully-boys."

But Buchanan had seen that they were paying him no attention at all. Instead, after a survey of the saloon, they began walking to the table where Ellen Booth and Juanita had just seated themselves. The tall man turned around, waited with his elbows resting on the bar at his back.

But their business wasn't with Juanita, either.

"Come on along with us, Mrs. Booth," Lafe said in a hard, carrying voice. "Sheriff Hallett wants to see you."

Ellen stared up at the deputy, her eyes bewildered.

"What for?" she asked. "What have I done?"

Lafe produced the warrant, handed it to her. She read the thing, and it might have been written in Sanskrit for all the meaning it had for her.

"It's a lie," she protested, throwing the paper on the table. "I haven't committed any crime."

Now little Birdy was going there, abandoning the advice he had just given.

"Here now, here now!" he said excitedly. "Hasn't Hallett troubled the girl enough for one day? You boys get out of my place!"

"Stand away from us, Birdy, before you get blown over," Lafe said.

"You don't scare me, Lafe Jenkins. You or your high-and-mighty boss . . ."

The one named Enos took Birdy's tie and collar in his fist, brought him forward and then shoved him backward. Birdy careened into a table and went sprawling to the sawdust-covered floor. Ellen gave a short cry, came out of her seat to go to him. Lafe's arm dropped in front of her and his hand tightened on her shoulder.

"You're under arrest, girlie. Let's get going." He spun her around roughly, began pulling her toward the doors. Birdy rose to one knee, went down again from Enos' boot against his thin chest.

"Hold it, friend," Buchanan called out and his voice sounded almost regretful. Lafe gave him a sidelong glance.

"What's your problem?"

"Damned if I know," Buchanan admitted, pushing away from the bar. The place had become very quiet and the sound of his bootheels was strangely casual as he approached the deputies.

"Back off," Enos said dangerously, stepping across his path.

"You boys run a hard town for the ladies," Buchanan said, moving in close. "What's this one getting pushed around for?"

"Climb back in your bottle," Enos told him and made the mistake of shoving him. Buchanan swung on reflexes alone, and Enos went down as if a tree had fallen on him. Lafe started backward, dragging Ellen with one hand, clawing at his holster with the other.

"Pull that gun," Buchanan warned him, "and I'll shove it down your throat."

Lafe's motion halted with the .45 half-drawn and his square face seemed perplexed.

"Stop it!" Ellen pleaded then. "Stop before someone is killed!" She twisted her body so that she was directly between the two men, who stood looking into each other's eyes like bull mastiffs.

"You're bracing the law, cowboy," Lafe said raggedly. "Move on back to that bar."

"Let's hear the charge against the lady."

"It don't have a goddam thing to do with you . . ."

"I'm her lawyer," Buchanan said, and though he was smiling it promised no friendship for Lafe Jenkins.

"No," Ellen said quickly. "No! Do as he says!"

"He'll take you on out of here then."

"Do as he says!" she repeated. "I don't want anyone killed because of me!"

"Go on," Lafe put in on his own. "Back off!"

The smile was gone from Buchanan's face. He looked gloomily undecided.

"Please!" Ellen said.

With that the tall man swung away, returned to his half-finished drink and washed his hands of the whole problem. Lafe spent the next several minutes getting his groggy partner erect and then they were gone. Birdy Warren joined Buchanan, his manner dejected.

"How do you like the law we got in this town?" he asked.

"Kind of hard to tell which is law and which ain't," Buchanan said and the man on his left touched his arm.

"You had a close call there, stranger," the man said.

"I did?"

"That Lafe's a man-killer. And fast as they come in these parts. Lucky for you the little gal spoke up like she did."

"Yeah," Buchanan said, laughing wryly. "This is about the luckiest day I ever spent in my life." He tossed off the drink, declined another from Birdy and crossed to where Juanita sat.

"Venga aquí, muchacha," he said.

"Where you off to?" Birdy called after him.

"See if my horse can ride," he told him and escorted the Mexican girl out onto the street. They walked for several moments in silence and then she spoke.

"Señor," she said, *"por favor, no me llama*

66

'*muchacha.*' I am a woman."

He looked down at her, critically. "I guess you're right at that," he said.

"*¿Qué dice?*"

"I said I won't call you a little girl."

"*Gracias.*"

They entered the dark livery and the sound of Doc Allen's voice came to them. Buchanan found him sitting comfortably in a stall with the mustang, who was feeding on the first oats she'd had in two weeks.

"Who you talking to?" Buchanan asked the vet, noting the third-empty bottle but no other person.

"Our ladyfriend," Allen answered. "Smartest listenin' animal I ever run across." He peered around Buchanan's legs. "You're bein' followed," he said.

"I know. How's the filly?"

"Well, she's minus one little stone. And she ain't runnin' a fever. I'd say she's fine." He pulled at the bottle. "Your friend there don't have much to say, does she?"

"Only in Mex. Can I ride to where I'm going?"

"In a couple of days. A week."

"Hell, I got to pull stakes now."

"Not on your life. Matter of fact, I think I'd shoot you in the back if you even put a saddle on her."

"How about late tonight?" Buchanan asked him. "If I take her real slow and gentle."

"Have to be *real* slow and gentle. And rest her every five, six miles."

"She could make it to Sacramento?"

"Leave her here a week and this girl will take you to Alaska. To the top of Alaska. And then swim you across to Russia."

Buchanan laughed at the man, felt a warmth for him in their common admiration for the horse.

"How much do I owe you, Doc?" he asked then.

"Birdy Warren settled my bill."

"The hell he did!"

"In full. Came in here babbling about you tangling with Bull Hynman. That sets you up mighty high with Birdy."

"Nothing doing. How much do I owe?"

"That's an awful pretty friend you collected for yourself," the vet said, changing the subject abruptly. "Makes it a nice trip to Sacramento."

"Except that she's going to Salinas."

"What in the world for?"

"That's where her people are." He was inspecting the hoof.

"All the more reason to go to Sacramento with you."

"Stick to horses, Doc," Buchanan said mildly. "What's the due bill on this one?"

"A month's free likker. Now stop talking about it." He gave the bottle another try. "Your filly's got good posture," he said. "What's her name?"

"Juanita, and she's not mine."

"What's she followin' you around for then?"

"I'm trying to get her a ride down to Salinas."

"Take my buggy."

Buchanan turned to the girl, asked her if she could drive a horse and buggy. She said she never had.

"She'd need somebody to take her," Buchanan explained to the vet.

"I'm your man," Allen said.

"And I'm serious."

"So am I, damn it. You think I don't know my way to Salinas?"

"Sure you do," Buchanan told him tactfully, "but you're needed right here." He signalled Juanita that they were leaving. "Can't thank you enough for the job, Doc," he said. "She looks just fine."

"Salinas," the old man muttered. "Get there in my sleep."

Which is how you would get there, Buchanan thought to himself as he took the girl back into the sunlight again. Out here he began to wonder in earnest what the hell he *was* going to do about her. Take her along to Sacramento . . . ?

"Why do you shake your head like that?" she asked him in her soft voice.

"To get rid of an idea. Listen, are you hungry?"

"Very much."

"Me too," he said, as if making a discovery. He put an arm around her shoulder. *"Vamos,"* he said cheerfully. "Let's hunt us a couple of thick steaks."

Chapter Six

Bull Hynman's shadowy career had not been without its setbacks and injuries, but he could not remember a time when he had been made to look so bad as on the second floor of the bordello. And when he had charged out of the place — head aching, jaw tender — his intention had been simply, savagely, to return to the office for a workable gun and empty it into the body of the saddle bum. But then he saw the sonofabitch talking to Birdy Warren and decided to take Lafe and Enos back with him in case the opposition was more than expected.

In any event, Hynman wanted to handle the business without Sid Hallett knowing about it. The sheriff wasn't the easiest man in the world to work for. He expected things just so, and Bull didn't want to have those eyes on him while he tried to explain that some drifter just walked in off the street and took the new girl away.

It was agitating, then, to meet Lafe and Enos riding to River Street on Hallett's business — and on top of his own personal problem to have to wonder what the boss wanted with Ellen Booth. Why the hell were things going wrong today, this quiet Sunday when he was supposed to have the afternoon and night off?

Nor did it go any better for him when he walked into the office for another gun. Hallett was sitting behind the desk, looking impatient, and his eyes grew sharp when he saw Hynman's face.

"What happened to you?"

"Nothin' much."

"Nothing *much?*"

"Had a run-in with somebody over on River Street. Got the drop on me."

"Who was it?"

Hynman shook his head. "Never saw him before," he growled. "But I'm headin' right back to fix his wagon."

"You put the girl in the house, though?"

Hynman's face, if possible, seemed even more pained. "For the time bein'," he answered lamely, "she's with this bushwhacker."

Sid Hallett came to his feet. "Describe him," he said tersely.

"Big bastard," Hynman said. "Busted nose, needs a shave. Thinks he's tough," he added as an afterthought.

Hallett reached into his desk, took out the letter from the prison warden and quickly scanned it.

"Is his name Reeves?" he demanded. "Luther Reeves?"

"Didn't catch his name," Hynman said. "You know him?"

"Read this," Hallett told him, handing over the letter. Hynman studied it, scowling, then looked up.

"I don't know," he said. "It could be the same

bird. Anyways, he's gonna be dead before the sun sets. Whoever he is."

"That may well be," Hallett said, "but he's going to tell me a few things first."

"What things?"

"Their plans — his and Frank Booth's. Booth doesn't think we know he has a partner. So he keeps himself out of sight and sends this other one to test our strength. I'm surprised he didn't kill you when he had the opportunity."

"He tried," Hynman said then. "Busted my gun with the shot."

"That proves it!" Hallett said. "When Lafe and Enos return I want the three of you to pick him up. Alive," he added. "I mean to find out what trouble Frank Booth has in mind."

"How come you sent them for his wife?" Hynman asked and Hallett smiled coldly.

"An ounce of prevention, Brother. With her in my custody I think that Booth will consider the consequences of his mischief."

"What's he comin' back to do?"

"I don't know," Hallett answered. "But I'm prepared for anything."

Hynman walked over to the gun-locker, rearmed himself with a Colt .45 and tested the trigger mechanism before loading it. For himself he wasn't sure at all that the man he was going to settle with was this Luther Reeves. The play inside Maude's had been pure ramstammer, not the actions of an ex-convict getting set to pull a job in town. But he couldn't tell the sheriff that, not without making himself look second-best, and so he'd have to hold off finishing the scudder until Hallett had his powwow.

The buggy pulled up outside and a moment later Lafe led Ellen Booth into the office. Enos followed. He, too, carried his own souvenir of the trip to Damnation — a tremendous purple bruise that all but closed his left eye.

Lafe spoke as soon as the door closed, his voice tight and angry.

"There's a guy in Birdy's just beggin' for it, Sheriff," he said.

"Throws a long shadow?" Hynman asked, staring at Enos' eye.

"That's him," Enos said. "And by God he's going to lie in it . . ."

"All right," Hallett said to Bull Hynman. "You've got your assignment. Be sure he's alive when you bring him back here."

Hynman nodded, let his glance shift to Ellen Booth's face, drop down over her figure hungrily. The girl's eyes flashed.

"I hear you met your match today," she told the deputy, getting the reaction she wished for in his changed expression.

"If that's what he's braggin' on," Hynman said hotly, "then he's gonna find out different . . ."

"I said all right," Hallett repeated. "Be on your way."

They trooped out of the office and Ellen swung to the grim law enforcer. "Why am I here?" she demanded. Hallett turned his back to her, walked around his desk and sat down. He did not invite her to take the other chair.

"I want to know why I was brought here!" Ellen said again.

"Did you read the warrant, Sister?" Hallett asked pontifically.

"I read it," she answered, "but it made no sense. If this has anything to do with those horrible things you accused me of in church — if you have one speck of proof that I've behaved sinfully . . ."

"We sin by thought and deed," Hallett interrupted. "You fell from the Lord's grace when you crossed the threshold of that house of wickedness."

"I think you're the one who sins by thought, Mr. Hallett," Ellen said. "I did nothing wrong by working for Birdy Warren."

"What's done is done, Sister," he said, raising his long bony hand as if to signify the gates of heaven had been shut forever against Ellen Booth. Then he lowered the hand, reached into his coat and almost casually produced the letter. "I want you to read this," he said, but Ellen had already recognized the handwriting and was reaching for it.

"This is addressed to me," she said.

"So it is."

"But it's been opened!"

"So it has. Read it, Sister."

Helpless anger jumped into the girl's eyes. "You

74

have no right to open my mail! It's against the law."

Hallett smiled sardonically. "Make a complaint to the sheriff," he advised her. "But first, read the letter."

She slid the note from the envelope, her fingers trembling from the outrage she felt. And as she dropped her gaze to read the message Hallett watched her face carefully, his features hawkish in their intensity. What she read — about her husband wanting her to go to San Francisco, his having business to attend to — washed away her anger, replaced it with a puzzled anxiety. She read it through another time, folded it into the envelope again and put it in the pocket of her dress.

"What do you think of it?" Hallett asked then. "What does your convict husband intend to do?"

"He is no longer a convict," Ellen pointed out quietly. "And he intends to meet me in San Francisco."

"I see. And what urgent business does he have, this man who has been imprisoned for the past three years?"

"What concern is that of yours?"

"I am sworn to uphold the law," he intoned. "It is my duty to prevent crime just as it is to bring criminals to the bar of justice."

"What crime? Frank has paid in full!"

"Ah, but has he repented in full, Sister? Or is his heart full of bitterness and sin?"

She stared at him. "What are you trying to say?" she asked.

"That Frank Booth has sold his immortal soul. He was devious in his crime before, cunning and circumspect. But now he has found a partner . . ."

"That's not true!"

"It is true." Hallett picked up the letter that Hynman had laid on the desktop. "This is from the warden at the penitentiary," he said. "Let me quote him. 'During the past year Frank Booth has formed a close friendship with another inmate, one Luther Reeves. Reeves is a large man, domineering of character, and with a well-earned reputation as a desperado. His previous record,' " Hallett continued, speaking more slowly, " 'includes desertion from the army, armed robbery — and rape.' " He paused there, lifted his eyes to Ellen's shocked face. Then he read on. " 'Reeves was sentenced to this institution for a bank holdup for a term of five years. He was released on June the third, this year. I include the above information for the reason that the Chief of Guards believes that Booth and Reeves plan to join forces following Booth's release and continue their criminal careers.' "

He finished, held out the letter for her to read. Ellen looked at it as if it were a coiled snake.

"Now what have you got to say?"

"I don't believe it. Frank wouldn't have anything to do with a — with a man like that."

"Then why is his rapist friend already on the scene?"

"*What?*"

"Oh, yes. He is the same man who tried to kill my deputy earlier. They have gone to River Street to capture him."

"No," Ellen said, her voice barely audible. Whatever else that man named Buchanan was, he was not any of the things described in the letter. A woman knew, her instincts warned her. If Buchanan was a formidable type, a gunman and a roughneck, she had not known a moment's fear of him because of her sex.

"No," she said again to Sidney Hallett. "You are making a mistake. He is not the man described in that letter."

"He is. And when I've questioned him I'll know where your husband is hiding himself, what he's up to. Then," Hallett said, "I'll deal with him as I should have in the beginning." As he spoke the last words the man's voice seemed to catch in his throat, emotionally, and the expression in his eyes was not entirely sane.

"What do you mean — in the beginning?"

"You were young," Hallett said. "You didn't know your own mind. He came here, from San Francisco. You were as innocent to resist temptation as Eve in the garden . . ."

"Stop it!" Ellen cried at him. "Stop such talk! That's what you said to my father nearly four years ago — and it's all a lie! I fell in love with Frank Booth. I married him of my own volition, willingly! There was no temptation, no seduction . . ."

Once again Hallett raised his arm, cutting off her protest.

"That is water under the bridge," he said. "What I had you brought in for was to tell you that you are not going to San Francisco. You are staying here."

"*Here?*" Ellen repeated. "Here in the jail?"

"For your own protection," Hallett told her. But he gave her a different reason than he had given Bull Hynman. "This time your husband intends you to be the receiver of stolen money."

"He wouldn't," she said loyally. "Frank wouldn't do that."

"You've forgotten his paramour?" Hallett chided. "What was the jezebel's name?"

"Ruby Fowler," Ellen said, automatically speaking a name that was never very far from her thoughts.

"Ruby Fowler," Hallett echoed. "His mistress. What an irony that she should betray him for another man — and that be his undoing."

Ellen looked down at her lap.

"So you will be the guest of the township," Hallett said. "For your own good."

"I can look after myself."

"No, you cannot look after yourself." The man stood up from the chair, rose to his impressive height above the girl. "Come along," he told her then and led the way through the adjoining door to the jail cells beyond. He pointed to the same one that the Mexican girl had occupied briefly earlier in the afternoon, and when Ellen entered it, despondently, he closed the iron door behind her and locked it.

The Sheriff of Salvation strode back across the room then, paused for a lingering moment at the door.

"This is for your own good," he said a second time. "No harm can come to you here."

Chapter Seven

Now what? old Pete Nabor wondered as he watched Hynman, Lafe and Enos canter past the hotel toward Damnation. The sheriff's men rode three abreast along Sinai Street, their faces rock-hard, stolidly ruthless, and anyone coming from the other direction would have had to pull aside for them or be run over.

Now what? the old man wondered, cursing the infirmity that rooted him to the rocking chair, kept him from tagging along to observe the happenings that he knew must be going on over at River Street. But what *was* happening? It was not a blessing but a torture to have a mind so bright and curious about the life all around him and a body no longer capable of exploring it.

He remembered very clearly the big man who had passed this way at high noon, a man with the wildness in him, and a concern for a misbegotten pony. And Ellen Booth went down that way a short time later, a suitcase in her hand, too distracted by the blow Sid Hallett had dealt her to give anything but a farewell nod of her head. Then Bull Hynman, that arrogant bully, driving the covered wagon. Hallett, himself, riding down Genesis Street at an unusual clip, returning. Lafe and Enos came by next, paused for an agitated conversation with Hynman — and the treat of seeing the Chief Deputy with that marvelous swelling along his jaw. Nabor even observed Hynman's empty holster, made himself a canny bet that somehow, for some reason, the big stranger was involved.

But whatever satisfaction he got from that disappeared when the other two came back with Ellen in their custody. Not even Enos' shiner could brighten the picture that conjured up.

What was going on? he wondered worriedly. He felt a premonition that whatever it was, Sidney Hallett was invincible in this little corner of the world. There was no surer sign of it than the set of the backs of the three troopers he was dispatching to River Street.

The three of them felt that way about it themselves, although Lafe Jenkins — who probably had all the imagination in the group — voiced an objection.

"How come we got to take him alive?" he asked Hynman.

"There's reasons," Hynman answered mysteriously, always jealous of his rank.

"There's reasons why somebody could get himself hurt, too," Lafe grumbled. Hynman looked at him.

"For all the rep you're supposed to have," he sneered, "I never saw such a cautious gunny."

"Like I told you, Bull," the other man said. "Any time, any place."

"It'll come sooner'n you expect, you don't quit lickin' Hallett's boots."

"How about right now?" Lafe said thinly, pulling in on his reins. Enos veered his own mount sharply, got between them.

"Cut it out!" he protested. "We all of us eat at the same trough. And we eat friggin' well good!"

The quarrelers looked at each other balefully, reflecting on the words of wisdom just spoken. They were all too true, for not anywhere west of Dodge were the pickings so good as in little, out-of-the-way Salvation, the town their boss carried around in his vest pocket.

"We got work to do," Bull Hynman said then. "Let's get it done with."

A man named Bones McGrath spread the word. He ran into the saloon, shouted the news in a breathless voice.

"Hallett's crew! Comin' this way!"

Birdy Warren came out from behind the bar, made a beeline for the back room where Buchanan and the girl were finishing their meal. He threw the door open.

"You got trouble," Birdy said. "Hallett's sent his boys."

Buchanan set down his mug of coffee. "Damnation," he said. "Ain't they got other work to do?" He pushed his chair back, stood up from the table. His glance fell on Juanita, full of concern.

"We got to hide her somewhere," he said to Birdy.

"There's a halfway sort of cellar under the bar," Birdy said. "It's dark and none too comfortable."

"Be some better than the bawdyhouse," Buchanan said. Then, to the girl: "You go with him. To hide yourself."

"No. I want to stay where you are."

Buchanan shook his head. "I'm going to be busy. Go on, now. *Pronto!*"

She hadn't heard that fiber in his voice before and her reaction was to obey instantly.

"How about you?" Birdy asked him.

"Best bet is to draw 'em away from here," Buchanan said, crossing to the open window. He threw a long leg over the sill, looked back into the room. "You sure got yourself some real law in this town," he commented.

"The worst," Birdy admitted.

"Well, do what you can for Juanita. And in case I don't make it, try to get her to Salinas safe and sound."

"Do my best," Birdy promised. "Good luck to you."

Buchanan waved, went out the window. He was in an alleyway now, between the saloon and the barber's, and the destination he had decided upon was the stable. With a little luck, he thought, it might be possible to hold them off there. With a little more luck he might even survive until nightfall, buy himself a riding chance to slip out of their damn town and never return.

But it was also necessary that they know he wasn't in Birdy's. Therefore he started out for the stable at a leisurely pace, in full view of anyone coming along River Street.

Lafe Jenkins spotted him almost immediately.

"Hold it, Rannie!" he ordered. "You're under arrest!"

Buchanan broke into a run. He ran unevenly, sprinting one moment, jogging the next, his tall body jackknifed to make it as difficult a target as he could. Ninety feet ahead loomed the brown, flat-roofed stable — but thirty yards of that was clearing, with no cover. As he angled his way across it he knew that he was giving his luck one hell of a test. Then he had the stable's big back door open and was inside, bolting the door shut with the four-foot beam that lay on the floor. This was the area where the smith worked — the familiar forge, the anvil, assorted hammers and iron shoes — and to one side was a wall-ladder that led to the loft above. Buchanan mounted it, unhurriedly, all his senses attuned to the sound of pursuit.

Halfway up the ladder he halted. *Where was the pursuit?* Here he'd taken a damn fool's own risk to show himself, made a sitting duck of himself. It suddenly dawned on Buchanan that not a shot had been fired. There had been that shout to halt, and following that nothing.

He finished the climb into the loft, thinking about it, crossed to the little window and looked down. They were there, three of them, badges glistening officiously on their shirtfronts. He couldn't hear what was being said, but the one he'd fought with in the brothel was waving off the one he'd belted in Birdy's a little while ago. That one rode his horse around to the front of the building, but not willingly.

Why hadn't they opened up on him when they had such a chance?

Buchanan considered himself a practical type of man. Not that he condoned the sad state of law and order in Salvation — that signpost, 'We are God-fearing and Law-abiding,' was somewhat misleading. But he understood, in his practical fashion, what this Sidney Hallett was trying to put over — understood why his deputies had to wipe out any interference before the idea became fashionable.

But there he'd been, running across that clearing, in their gunsights for a long ten seconds, and not one crack had they taken at him. A practical man doesn't like the unorthodox. Buchanan was bothered by the realization that they hadn't come to kill him but to take him alive. Bothered because it put him at a disadvantage, morally speaking.

For how could you pull a trigger on a man if he didn't intend the same?

But that didn't change the fact that they had come at him. 'Under arrest' they said. For what? Was it always this Hallett's game that was played?

The hell with that, Buchanan told himself and broke the pane of glass with his gunbarrel. Bull

Hynman and Lafe Jenkins looked upward sharply, in surprise. Then their horses reared and nearly threw them as Buchanan threw down two wicked shots at their feet. And still they kept their guns bolstered.

"Either fight or go on home," he called out. "I got better things to do."

"Come down outta there, you bastard."

Buchanan let loose two more shots, even closer. "Give it up, boys," he advised them. "I might miss next time and drop you both."

They dismounted, faces furious, found the door bolted tight and started around front.

"Some goddam job this is gonna be," Lafe complained angrily.

"Whatta you want me to do about it?" Bull growled back at him. "The boss wants to talk to him."

Enos had entered the stable and been confronted by Doc Allen. The vet had worked his way well down on the bottle of corn and his eyes were bleary.

"Can't arrest me," he told the deputy. "Immune to the law."

Enos brushed him aside, started for the rear of the building and suddenly stopped short at the sound of firing from the loft overhead. He heard the man tell them to go home.

"What's that?" Allen asked. "What's goin' on?"

"Keep out of the way," Enos said to him. "Go somewheres and sleep it off."

There were two more shots, then it was quiet. A few moments later Hynman and Jenkins entered.

"Thought he might of plugged you," Enos said. "Bull, how you figure to get him down outta there?"

"Who?" Doc Allen asked. "Down outta where?"

"Me, Doc," Buchanan answered from above. He was standing on the loading platform, straddle-legged, all but inviting the sheriff's men to have a try at him.

"What you been up to?" Allen asked. "What'd you do?"

"Don't know."

"Come on down," Bull Hynman ordered. "Sheriff wants to ask you some questions."

"About what?"

"About Frank Booth."

"Never heard of him."

"You're a liar!"

"Not about any Frank Booth, I'm not."

"Your handle is Luther Reeves, ain't it?"

"Nope."

Hynman turned to the vet. "You know him," he said. "What's his name?"

Allen opened his mouth to answer, then looked puzzled. "What *is* your name, anyhow?" he called up to the platform.

"Buchanan, Doc. Alpine, West Texas."

"His name is Buchanan," Allen reported to Hynman. "And I can vouch for him. Any man that feels like he does for that horse over there is all right."

The sentence seemed to hang in the air, and it was as if Lafe Jenkins and Buchanan got the idea at the same time. For Buchanan's .45 jumped into his hand just as Lafe darted under the protruding platform and out of the other man's vision.

"Don't do it," Buchanan said warningly.

"Your filly's in my gunsights, Rannie," Lafe answered. "Come on down here."

"You'll be trading your friends for her," Buchanan said. "And yourself, so help me God."

"Watch close," Lafe said. "At five she gets it. Right in the belly. One," he counted. "Two. Three . . ."

"Coming down," Buchanan said, his voice sad.

"Throw the gun and belt first," Bull Hynman said then, miffed that Jenkins had made the play. "And move quick." Buchanan holstered the Colt, unfastened the belt and dropped the rig to the stable floor. He came down himself, and when he got there walked to Lafe Jenkins and stood gazing at him silently.

"I guess you would have at that," he said to him finally.

Then Doc Allen tried to shout a warning, but Bull Hynman was moving too quickly. He stepped in behind Buchanan and swung his gun savagely against the base of the tall man's skull. Buchanan's knees buckled, he half-turned around, and Hynman hit him again alongside the temple. Still he wouldn't go down.

"Watch out," Enos snarled and drove his fist into the pit of Buchanan's stomach. Buchanan grabbed for him and Hynman smashed the gun across the bridge of his nose. He fell face forward to the floor and Enos kicked him hard.

"Why, hell," Hynman said. "He ain't so tough."

It took the three of them to drag him out of the stable, and in full view of the onlookers Buchanan's wrists were lashed behind his back. The rope was then used to bind his ankles and the free end was made fast to Hynman's saddlehorn. All of this was done at Hynman's direction; he was determined to reassert himself. Now he mounted up, dragged the half-conscious Buchanan to the saloon entrance.

"Where's the girl?" he asked Birdy Warren.

"Gone to Salinas," Birdy answered worriedly.

"And you're a liar. I come back for him and I'll come back for her. Don't get in my way." With that he swung the horse around, started off down dusty River Street at a trot: the punishment that inflicted had the added effect of reviving the man at the end of the rope. Buchanan was well aware of his pain, but he'd been worked on before — by Mexicans — and he could live with that when he had to. The real hurt was in the thing itself, the degradation. They came into Sinai Street — peaceful, quiet Sinai — and Pete Nabor watched them ride past, saw his gloomy prophecy about the stranger come true.

Sid Hallett came out of his office to greet them, stood looking down at Buchanan incuriously, as if that were not another human being there but some captured animal. And Buchanan, for his own part, was just as expressionless.

"So this is the notorious Luther Reeves," the sheriff said.

"Claims to be somebody else," Bull Hynman said.

"Does he?"

"Speak your piece," Hynman said to Buchanan, prodding the blood-smeared face with the toe of his boot.

"My name is Buchanan," he told them all, his gaze fixed on Hynman. "And I'm going to fix you."

Bull laughed, brought his boot back. Hallett stopped him with a gesture.

"Not out here," he said sharply. "Bring him into the jail."

Enos untied his ankles, Lafe and Hynman hauled him to his feet, shoved him on into the office and to the jail section. Ellen Booth looked up as they came in, grimaced in horror at the condition of their prisoner. Amazingly, he grinned at her.

"I bruise easy," he said and she even smiled herself, reminded of the other time he'd said that. But then Sid Hallett spoke.

"Your husband's accomplice," he announced. "What do you think of him?"

"Do you know Frank?" Ellen asked in a quiet voice and Buchanan shook his head. "Were you ever in Marysville?"

"No."

She turned to Hallett. "I believe him," she said.

"Naturally," Hallett said, still sublimely confident that he had made no mistake. "Lafe, take Mrs. Booth into the office while we talk to this desperado." Jenkins unlocked the cell, held the door ajar.

"You're going to beat him again," she accused.

"No," Hallett said. "Not if he tells the truth about himself and your husband."

"He has told the truth. He doesn't know Frank . . ."

Hallett motioned impatiently with his head and Lafe took Ellen into the office, closed the door behind him.

"Now then," Hallett said to Buchanan, casually, as if Enos hadn't moved behind the bound man, pinioning his arms. As if Bull Hynman wasn't smoothing a buckskin glove over his knuckles. "Now then," Hallett said. "I say you are Luther Reeves."

"No," Buchanan said and Hynman hit him in the kidney.

"I say you came here with Frank Booth . . ."

"No." Hynman hit him in the same spot.

". . . to rob the bank," Hallett went on. "To kill me. Reeves, where is Booth right now?"

"Don't know," Buchanan said, but when he tried to ride with Hynman's driving fist the man

91

at his back kneed him hard.

"Luther," Hallett said, "this is painful to me. Especially on the Sabbath. Where is Frank Booth?"

Buchanan found himself bleeding from within. His throat was filling with it and a thin stream trickled from the corner of his mouth.

"Speak up, Brother," Hallett said and Hynman punched him again, monotonously. Buchanan's chin fell against his chest, his whole big body sagged. Enos had to let him fall.

Hynman dropped to one knee beside him, began rifling the pockets of his trousers. He found two ten-dollar gold pieces, some silver, an uncashed draft on the bank in Sacramento and a folded envelope.

"Let's see that letter," Hallett said and Hynman handed it to him, began pocketing the money for himself. The envelope had been originally addressed to 'Tom Buchanan, Town of Alpine, West Texas,' and someone there had forwarded it to 'The Tucker Ranch, El Paso.' But Buchanan had apparently moved on from that job and the third address was a rooming house in Yuma, a long five-hundred miles west. Frowning, Hallett took out the letter from the much-traveled envelope. He read:

Dear Friend Tom:

We are going to build a railroad up here called the Central Pacific and there is a job open for a boss troubleshooter. Believe me, you will be busy.

The pay is $100 a month, and I can promise you a fine future in railroading providing you live through it.

Come as soon as you can as there is a great deal of trouble to attend to. Enclosed find draft for $50.

Your old pal,
JACK MAGUIRE

Hallett refolded the letter, put it back in the envelope. "Return his belongings to him," he told Hynman in a stern voice.

"Return 'em?"

"You've made a mistake, Bull. This man isn't Luther Reeves."

Hynman started to set the record straight on that, but the look in Hallett's face warned him to let it ride.

"Even if he ain't Reeves," he did say, "that don't change what he did over on River Street. Not gonna let him get away with that, are you?"

Sid Hallett, for once, didn't know what he was going to do. Everyone in this part of the country knew of Jack Maguire and the new railroad, of the influence Maguire wielded in the capital city. Hallett had run things in Salvation without interference from Sacramento, but if Maguire started to check his friend's back trail there could be trouble aplenty.

On the other hand — and this was what bothered

him — how could he blithely send the fellow on his way, pretend nothing had happened to him? Damn Hynman anyhow for creating this problem when he had the real Luther Reeves and Frank Booth to worry about.

"Take that rope from his wrists," he ordered irritably. "Then lay him down in the other cell. We'll keep him here until I've figured out what to do about this blunder you led me into."

"Ah, he don't count for nobody," Hynman protested. "Let's try him for somethin' and hang the bastard."

"You're a fool!" Hallett told him in a scathing voice. "I never realized until now how big a fool you really are."

"Now wait a minute, Sid —"

" 'Sid'?" Hallett exploded. "To you I am 'Sheriff.' *Sheriff* Hallett. Pick that fellow up and put him on the cot, as I told you to."

Hynman and Enos obeyed, struggling with their outsize burden. Even as they did, and despite his annoyance, Hallett wondered if his deputy's solution might not be the best. Try this Buchanan for some crime, something heinous, and hang him. . . .

Why not? An offense so dishonorable that the railroad would want to wash its hands of the man completely. . . .

"Where is the Mexican girl now?" he asked Hynman. "With Maude?"

"Not yet," Hynman said, still smarting from the brief tongue-lashing he'd gotten. "I think

Birdy Warren's hiding her out in his place."

"Go get her. Bring her back here."

"Here?"

"I'm holding court," Hallett said, blandly assuming the idea for his own. "The girl is the complaining witness."

"She don't savvy no English."

"I know that. And on your way out tell Lafe to bring Mrs. Booth inside." Hynman left the jail and a moment later Jenkins and Ellen Booth re-entered it. Her eyes went immediately to the cell next to her own, lingered pityingly on the body sprawled lifeless-looking along the narrow cot.

"Did you get your truth?" she asked Hallett contemptuously.

"You seem quick to defend the man," Hallett replied. "Is it that you find yourself attracted to every scoundrel who comes along?"

"You accuse him," Ellen said. "That doesn't make it so."

"He confessed."

She eyed the gaunt man warily. "Confessed to what?"

"Abduction and lewd assault," Hallett said without a change in expression. "He took a Mexican girl from lawful custody . . ."

"You mean Juanita?" Ellen interrupted.

"What do you know of her?"

"I know that he got her out of that — that house," Ellen told him. "And he had to fight that ugly deputy of yours to do it."

95

"So that's the River Street version, is it? Well, this time justice will be done. He has confessed before witnesses."

"The same deputy? Is he one of the witnesses?"

"Put her in the cell," Hallett told Jenkins. "Then come to the office." He walked out and was seated behind the desk, writing names on a sheet of paper, when Jenkins joined him. "Do you know these six men, Lafe?" he asked, handing him the list. Jenkins studied it, nodded his head.

"The oldest gaffers in town," he said.

"I'd call them our senior citizens," Hallett said. "Venerable and respected."

Lafe shrugged. "Sure," he said. "Call 'em anything."

"Tell me — do any of those six speak or understand Spanish?"

Lafe looked it over again. "No," he said, "I don't think so. A couple of 'em, Davis and Clark, don't understand much of anything anymore."

"Responsible men, though. God-fearing. I want you to round them up, bring them to the church. Those who, ah, can't ride I want you to transport in the buggy."

"Sure," Lafe said. "You having a special service tonight?"

"A trial," Hallett explained. "That's the jury."

Jenkins smiled knowingly and went to get the six old men who didn't speak Spanish.

Chapter Eight

Out of the clear blue sky of a summer Sunday a man named Buchanan had walked into the little world of little Birdy Warren — and Birdy had thought him invincible. But now, if he closed his eyes, Birdy saw his nonpareil being trussed hand and foot, dragged through the dust like a common thief. And without even giving them a fight for it. That was what dismayed Birdy, the recreation in his mind of that shameful moment when Buchanan's reckless courage had deserted him and he'd surrendered.

"Don't take it to heart so, boss," his bartender Sam told him. "That fella was just an odds-player is all."

"What?"

"What I mean is, he braced Bull Hynman and didn't get kilt. Then he braces Lafe and Enos and still don't get kilt. This time he must've figured it was their turn to win a pot so he throws in his hand . . ."

"Pull that shirt down from over the mirror," Birdy said. "Pull it down and burn it."

"Sure, boss," Sam said, taking Buchanan's blood-stained shirt from its place of honor and tossing it negligently into the trash barrel with the cigar butts and empty whisky bottles. "You ain't forgot that Hynman's comin' back to pay a visit?"

"I ain't forgot."

"What you plannin' to do?"

"Spit in his eye, that's what," Birdy said and filled his glass for the third time in the past thirty minutes.

"I'd give that idea some careful thought," the chubby bartender advised. "I wouldn't buy myself no grief from that hombre."

"A goddam bully-boy. He ain't so much."

"Enough to drag that fella out by his heels," Sam reminded him. "You ought to play the percentages, too."

"Whatta you mean?"

"Hell, boss, she's only a Mex . . ."

"And what're you? What am I? Because she don't talk our lingo, you think she don't *feel*? You got a sweet little daughter: you want her thrown into Maude's?"

"Simmer down, boss . . ."

"Simmer down, hell! Besides that, I made a promise to look out for her."

"Look out for yourself, I always say," Sam said and then his voice trailed away as the doors parted and a fiercely glowering Bull Hynman entered the place. Birdy, cued by his bartender's frightened face, took the dutch courage in his glass and swung around. Hynman bore down on him as relentlessly as a storm cloud.

"I come for the woman," he said, "and I got no time for palaver. Where is she?"

"Gone," Birdy answered unevenly, fighting to keep his voice unafraid. "Gone to Salinas like I said."

"Just one more time, little man. Where is she?"

"Gone to —" Hynman's fingers went around his slender neck, choking all sound.

"This is the day," Hynman said, "when we teach you boys about the law in Salvation." His grip tightened and Birdy's eyes looked sick. "Where is she?" Hynman asked.

"Salinas," Birdy said in a strangling voice. Hynman pulled back his other fist to smash the helpless face below him.

"She's in the cellar!" Sam shouted. "Down here!" He pointed frantically at the trap door beneath the bar, reached down to pull it open. Hynman thrust Birdy Warren away from him, walked around behind the bar. Crouched in the storage cellar, her face a study in terror, was Juanita. She had recognized Hynman's deep voice, and at sight of him she screamed.

It sounded pitiful to everyone but Bull Hynman, who laughed.

"Ain't forgot me, huh?" he asked her, then motioned with his hand. "Come on up, sweetie," he said. "Let's have a look at ya."

She knew what he meant but she cowered there, petrified. Hynman went down the short flight of steps, pulled her out by the arm. Birdy was with them then, trying to intervene, and Hynman knocked him down with a backhanded sweep. There was no other opposition in the saloon and the deputy left the place.

Lafe Jenkins, meantime, was out beating the bushes for Hallett's 'blue ribbon' jury. Everywhere he went he was greeted with trepidation and misunderstanding. Seventy-year-old Cy Taylor thought the sheriff's man was here to foreclose, it having slipped his tired mind that he had clear title to the homestead for the past five years. Ab Davis and Josh Clark, both crowding eighty, let themselves be put into the buckboard under the vague impression that they were under arrest. The three other jurors, none of whom could see too well or hear too well, made it to the church under their own power.

Hallett greeted them there, grave of mien, solemn of voice, and escorted each to a seat on the front bench. Then, using the Holy Bible as a prop in the farce he was about to perpetrate, he had them all swear an oath 'to see that justice was done, without fear or favor, so help him God.'

"What all's happened, Reverend?" old Andy Southworth asked in a wavering voice, using Hallett's alternate title because of the surroundings.

"There's been a shocking crime committed in our midst today, Brother," Hallett answered him. "A crime against a defenseless young woman . . ."

"You caught the critter?"

"We have him in custody."

"Then let's stretch his neck and go home."

"No, Brother," Hallett said. "Not until this

sworn jury has heard the evidence and judged his guilt. A fair trial for all in Salvation."

"What'd he say?" Ab Davis asked his neighbor.

"There's gonna be a trial."

"What?"

"A *trial.*"

Hallett moved to where Davis sat, leaned over the railing.

"Brother Davis," he asked in a strong voice, "do you speak Mexican?"

The old man looked at him blankly for a moment, then shook his head. Hallett glanced up and down the panel.

"Anybody speak or understand Mexican?" he asked. None of them did and Hallett turned to the side, where Hynman stood with Juanita. "Bring the accusing witness in," he called and Hynman pushed the bewildered, doe-eyed girl before him, halted her before a straight-backed chair that had been placed a long twenty feet from the jurors.

"Brothers," Hallett intoned, "this is the poor unfortunate female who was dishonored over on River Street."

"She looks scared to death," Juror Southworth observed.

"Ay," Hallett said smoothly, "her trust in all men has been shaken. Would you believe it — she's even afraid of me?"

"Don't you worry none, missy," Southworth tried to tell her. "You got nothin' to fear now . . ."

"She speaks no English, Brother," Hallett said. "I'll translate what you told her." He turned to Juanita, who took an involuntary step backward. "These men are judges," he said in her own language. "They are going to help you."

Her face showed that she plainly didn't believe him.

"You want to go home, don't you?" Hallett said then.

She nodded. "Yes," she said very quietly.

"*Siéntese,*" Hallett told her. "Over there. And when I ask a question you will answer me. "*¿Comprende usted?*"

"*Sí,*" Juanita said, not understanding what was going on at all in this living nightmare that had begun at noon. Now the evil man who was the cause of everything bad had turned to the old ones he called the judges and was speaking to them in the Yanqui tongue.

"She understands now that you are here to see that justice is done," Hallett was saying to them, taking note that Josh Clark was dozing. "I'll have her tell what happened in her own words."

"But we can't understand a word," Southworth said.

"I'll explain, Brother, as we go along," Hallett assured him, swinging around to Juanita. "*Dígalos que pasa,*" he said. "From the beginning."

"*¿Todo?*"

"Yes, everything."

Juanita, looking surprised, told them everything. She began by pointing at Hallett and describing him as the worst man in the world. *Un diablo.*

"She says that I have been a great help to her," Hallett translated.

Juanita told them about the character of Bull Hynman then, about him taking her to the bordello for a sinful purpose.

"She's grateful to Deputy Hynman, too," Hallett explained to the jury. Now Ab Davis had fallen asleep.

Juanita came to Buchanan, raised her arm toward the high ceiling. Tall as a cypress, he was, and strong as oak. But a man of honor, and kind. He saved her from Hynman.

"She was attacked by a hulking brute," Hallett translated. "His name is Buchanan. Deputy Hynman captured the scoundrel . . ."

"Is *that* what she just said?" Andy Southward asked doubtfully.

"That is what she just said," Hallett told him. "What did you think she said, Brother?"

"Well," the old man said, then shook his head. "Nothin'," he finished lamely.

"*Dígalos,*" Hallett said to the Mexican girl. "Tell them the rest."

"But that is the worst of it," Juanita protested reasonably, "and they sit there and do nothing. Two of them even sleep . . ."

"Then you have nothing more to say?"

"I think this is some kind of a trick. And what have you done with Señor Buchanan?"

103

"Now what's she sayin', Reverend?" South-worth inquired.

"The young woman is concerned that there won't be justice done on her behalf. She asks for the supreme penalty."

"Has she identified the dog?" Southworth asked and Hallett's face became thoughtful. He had mis-judged this particular senior citizen and now there was an element of risk in what should have been a cut-and-dried situation.

"Of course she's identified him," he said.

"Well, I'm no lawyer or nothin' like that," Southworth countered, "but I think she oughtta point him out right here in front of the jury."

Hallett gazed at him coldly, then turned to Bull Hynman.

"Get the prisoner," he said. "Lafe," he added, "you better go along."

For the first quarter-hour after she had been put back in the cell, Ellen Booth could not be really sure if the man lying on the other cot was still alive. Then he groaned, deep inside his chest, and after another five minutes she saw his hand move, the long fingers closing slowly into a fist, then opening again. His enormous shoulders stirred beneath the tight shirt after that, and he raised his great shaggy head and rolled it round and round, as if testing that it was still joined to his neck.

"Is there anything I can do for you?" Ellen asked gently, then was sorry she'd spoken, for now he had to change the position of his body to look at her. The effort seemed tremendous.

"You could shoot me," Buchanan said. "I'd thank you for that."

"How can men be so brutal?" she wondered aloud. "So senselessly cruel."

Buchanan said nothing, kept experimenting with joints and muscles.

"Sidney Hallett is insane," Ellen said. "He belongs in Bedlam."

That barber knew his business, Buchanan decided, feeling the bandage still intact after all the dragging around and manhandling. *And those deputies knew theirs. Man, oh, man, what a bellyache . . .*

"Why did they pick on you so?" Ellen asked him.

"Their feelings were hurt," he said, finding that even to talk was uncomfortable.

"Because you helped that poor girl?"

"Or something," Buchanan said, wanting to be polite to a fellow prisoner but wishing she would let the conversation go until another time.

"I'll leave you be," Ellen said understandingly.

"That's all right," he said. "Talk if you want to."

But she fell silent, and the seconds seemed to drag on uncomfortably.

"Talk some more," Buchanan said at last. "You've got a nice voice."

Ellen gave a self-conscious little laugh. "Now I don't know what to talk about," she told him.

"Yourself," he suggested.

"Nothing to tell."

"Sure there is."

"It's mostly unhappy," she said. "You've got pain enough."

Buchanan had been working slowly to get all the way over on his back. Now he made it, and the release of pressure around his ribs made him sigh almost contentedly.

"How many laws did you break?" he asked the girl next door.

"None that I know about. I'm here as a kind of hostage for my husband."

Buchanan turned his head to look at her.

"It's true," she told him. "That's the reason I'm here."

Buchanan considered it, filed it in his mind with all the goings-on. "I been one place and another," he said musingly. "Good places and bad. But I got to hand it to 'em in this town for pushiness."

"And nothing can be done about it."

He had no comment about that, nothing he wanted to put into words. He looked away from her, stared reflectively at the ceiling overhead.

"If only I could warn Frank, somehow," Ellen said.

"Frank?"

"My husband."

"Oh," Buchanan said. "So that's who Frank is." He smiled wryly. "Feel like I know him well," he said. "Him and his pal Luther."

"Don't say that, please," Ellen said. "Frank

106

wouldn't be friends with a man like that."

"Pretty bad actor, is he?"

"From his prison record," she said, "he must be terrible."

"Sure got the High Sheriff nerved-up something fierce," Buchanan said, idly massaging his tender stomach muscles. "Is your husband due to arrive real soon?"

"No," Ellen said with some warmth. "That's another of Hallett's weird guesses. Frank wrote and told me to meet him in San Francisco. I guess he wants to start all over again in a new place."

"He get in trouble here?"

She nodded. "At the bank," she said sadly.

"Held it up, did he?"

"No," she said. "He — misused some funds."

She didn't want to talk about it, Buchanan saw, and the subject was none of his business. But he still couldn't keep his mind from wondering if the sheriff might not be right in expecting company.

"Are you married?" Ellen asked him, so unexpectedly that a laugh burst from his throat. "Is it so funny for a man to have a wife?" she asked then.

"It wouldn't be funny for this man's wife, I tell you," he assured her. "It'd be real sad."

"Oh, maybe not," she said. "If you took some care of yourself you'd be presentable."

Buchanan's grin was mischievous. "I got to watch that pretty careful," he said.

"Watch what — being presentable?"

"Tried it down in 'Paso, just a couple of months ago. Got ahead a few dollars and bought myself the whole outfit. Silk shirt, string tie, frock coat, striped pants —" He broke off into an expansive sigh at the memory.

"You must have looked real nice," Ellen told him seriously.

"Nearly got myself killed, that's how nice."

"Killed?"

"Just did beat 'em out of town."

"Who?"

"The Vigilantes. Husbands, every last one of 'em." He shook his head. "I learned my lesson about being presentable," he said.

"You made the whole thing up," Ellen told him, smiling herself.

"Half, anyhow."

"Which half?" she said, and now there was mischief in her.

"Well, I did own the silk shirt," he admitted.

"What happened to it?"

"You ever hear of a thing called 'baccarat'?"

"No."

"Me neither," Buchanan said. "But I moved over from 'Paso to Yuma and there was a little fella there from New Orleans. French fella name of Andre that liked to have drunk me under the table." He stopped, looked at her. "You bored?" he asked.

She returned the glance, shook her head. "No," she said. "I'm not bored, but I don't know whether to believe you or not."

"Oh, this happened," he said regretfully. "What I did was, I packed my dude outfit real careful and drug it clear to Yuma. Figured the silk shirt and all might come in useful when I got to San Francisco . . ."

"You're going there, too?"

"Someday," Buchanan said. "I keep starting out for 'Frisco, but something keeps happening."

"What happened in Yuma?" Ellen asked.

"Baccarat," he answered simply. "That damn — beg your pardon . . ."

"It's all right."

"A man gets on the trail by himself," Buchanan apologized, "and his manners get shot to hell —" He caught himself up abruptly and in the sudden silence they both laughed spontaneously.

The door to the jail burst open and the guard Enos stood there with an astonished expression.

"What's goin' on in here?" he demanded suspiciously. "What you two up to?"

His entrance killed the lightheartedness in the room as surely as a wet blanket over a campfire. Buchanan raised his head from the cot, stared at the face of the man in the doorway as if he wanted to be sure not to ever forget a single feature.

Enos looked uncertain, brushed the butt of his gun with his hand, and then seemed to realize that he was in no danger at all. With that he hunched his shoulders, strode forward truculently and stopped at the barred cell.

"You got something to say, say it," he said.

Buchanan smiled at him, cheerlessly. Enos' own face hardened.

"Ain't had enough yet, have you?" he asked.

Buchanan's smile became wintrier still.

"Well, you listen then," Enos said, relishing what he had to tell him. "You listen to this. The sheriff's fixin' your wagon good. Oh, Jesus, are you gettin' it!"

The goading had no effect on the intended victim at all. The one it did get to was Ellen Booth.

"What do you mean, he's 'getting it'?" she demanded stridently. "All he ever did to you was knock you down — and you deserved that, if you ask me . . ."

"Nobody *is,* sister. Nobody's askin' *you* about anything."

"Bullies," she told him. "Just a gang of bullies."

"We're keepin' the law," Enos said. He swung his head to Buchanan again. "We're takin' care of the scudders who try to buck the law."

"How?" the girl said angrily. "What are you going to do to him?"

Enos leered down into Buchanan's face, made a giggling sound. "You're on trial," he said, trying to contain his mirth. "A judge, a jury, the whole shebang. And you know what that jury's goin' to do to you?" He waited, but no one else spoke. "That jury," Enos said, "is goin' to hang you. Hang you by the neck." He paused again, and then his eyes flickered impatiently at the lack of response from Buchanan. He turned away,

110

walked back to the doorway and turned again.

"So keep right on smilin'!" the deputy fairly shouted across the space. "I wanna see that look on your face when that rope hits your goddamn neck!" He went out, slamming the door behind him.

And leaving a quiet that lasted some five seconds.

"Well, anyhow," Buchanan said conversationally, "this little French fella cleaned me out. My money, my tack, that fancy shirt . . ."

"*Didn't you hear what he said?*" Ellen asked brokenly. "Hallett is going to *hang* you!"

Buchanan shrugged.

"But they can't! You haven't done a thing yet that was wrong."

"Haven't hung me yet, either," Buchanan pointed out.

The blonde girl had no ready answer to that, and as she looked at him her thoughts became very confused. A telltale flush spread into her cheeks. It was very unseemly, she told herself, to show such concern. As a married woman she had a code of behavior to follow, a strict one, and regardless of what she felt about any injustices done it hardly became her to associate on familiar terms with a man who was, after all, a total stranger. In this new frame of mind she began to magnify the words they had spoken, found something to be almost ashamed about in the easy laughter that had passed between them, the defense she had put up for him. And she was worried

111

that he might have gotten a mistaken idea about her sense of what was proper.

"You'd have liked that Frenchman," Buchanan happened to say then, his own mind still full of his misadventures in the town of Yuma. "Started dealing that baccarat and left me about as naked as the day I was born —" He broke off at the look in her face. "What's the matter?" he asked.

"I don't think we should talk like this," Ellen said stiffly.

"Like what?" he asked in surprise.

"Oh, so free and easy like," she told him. "Your stories might not be fit for a married lady's hearing."

Buchanan was puzzled to hear that for he had been careful to avoid mention of the girls he and Andre had met during that memorable two weeks of their friendship. And he had only spoken in the first place to help take her mind off her own troubles.

Probably just as well, though, he thought, *not to get too friendly under the circumstances.* They lived in two different worlds, had two different problems, and it might be high time to start thinking seriously about getting himself out of this rat-trap jail.

So he thought about it, not too successfully, and conversation lapsed between them. Then Hynman and Lafe Jenkins arrived.

"On your feet, bum," Buchanan was told, and after some deliberation he decided to get up from the cot, if for no other reason than to test his health. He stood there unsteadily, arms limp at his sides. Hynman seemed to be gauging him before he finally fished the key from his pocket and opened the cell door.

"Come on outta there," Hynman said and the tall man stepped forward. *Not yet,* he had decided. *You're not loose enough to make your play just yet.*

"Better tie his wrists, Bull," Lafe advised.

"What the hell for?" Hynman replied jeeringly.

"So's he don't try nothing," Lafe said.

"Well I hope, by Jesus, he does!"

"That ain't what Sid sent us for," Lafe pointed out then and that gave Hynman a moment's pause. From a nail on the wall he took a length of rope and fastened Buchanan's hands behind his back. Lafe held the connecting door open and Buchanan started for it.

"Mister," Ellen Booth called and he looked back over his shoulder at her. "I — I want to wish you luck," she said.

"And the same to you."

"Now ain't that touchin'," Hynman said and shoved Buchanan through the doorway, with such vehemence that Buchanan wondered about it. Damned if this ape didn't act like he had some interest in the girl. If he did she would probably need something more than luck.

He was taken out into the street, where it was twilight now, and loaded onto the rear of the buckboard with Jenkins for a guard. The wagon rolled along Sinai, took the turn up Genesis and pulled in before the church.

He was led inside the darkening building. The first person he saw was Juanita, with the menacing form of Hallett close beside her.

Ah, hell, Buchanan thought dismally.

Juanita gave a cry of recognition, would have come toward him but for Hallett's restraining hold on her arm.

"This is what I wanted to avoid," he told the jurymen. "The sight of him upsets her badly."

Andy Southworth peered up at the mauled prisoner and winced involuntarily. For a moment there he had thought the Mexican was glad to see him, but he knew now that no young girl in her right mind could possibly be happy to see the likes of that.

"Let's get the identifyin' over and done with quick," he suggested.

"Very well," Hallett said. "You two deputies stand on either side of the accused. I'll ask the witness to point out the man who attacked her." With that he turned to Juanita. *"Tenga cuidado,"* he cautioned her. "This is very important. Point to the man who helped you this afternoon."

Juanita seemed frightened and undecided.

"Do you want to help him?" Hallett asked sternly.

"Sí," she said. *"Muy mucho."*

"Then point to him so the judges will know which one he is."

Juanita's arm came up very slowly and she pointed her finger squarely at Buchanan.

"That's enough for me," Southworth an-

114

nounced. "Let the jury vote."

Buchanan looked at the old man who had spoken, at the line of even older men in the bench alongside him, and wondered what kind of foolishness they thought they were about. He watched as three of them were awaked from sound sleep and began conferring all around. Then they were quiet.

"Have you reached your verdict?" Hallett asked.

"We sure have, Reverend. He's guilty as charged and ought to be strung up at the crack of dawn."

"Hold on there," Buchanan protested. "*Who's* guilty as charged?"

"You are, you damn dirty skunk!" Southworth shouted at him.

"Wait a minute, old-timer. You and your friends've been flim-flammed in here —" Hallett was bearing down on him, waving his arms, and Hynman was swinging the familiar gun with the same hard accuracy. Buchanan would have taken still another fall except that both deputies were holding him erect, turning him around and dragging him away.

And in the unexpected diversion Juanita saw her chance and made a break for it, out the back door of the church and into the gathering gloom of Genesis Street.

Chapter Nine

It was not possible, Hallett kept telling his harassed deputies that night, for a good-looking Mexican girl in a distinctive black dress to disappear within the precincts of Salvation. The search for her had been instituted as soon as Buchanan had been remanded to his cell, with all three deputies fanning out over the countryside, questioning everyone they met, returning empty-handed.

She had not had time to reach River Street, not on foot, but Bull Hynman had ridden there immediately. He had taken Birdy's place apart, he reported, and she was not hiding there. He had searched the livery with a lantern from top to bottom, gone through the other stores — even made a wild room-to-room search of Maude's in the hope that the girl might have returned to the very place she was trying so desperately to escape.

Lafe and Enos had gone over Sinai and Genesis Streets as carefully as they knew how, gone out of town over every possible trail she might have followed, returned to the office of the stormy-faced sheriff to report no sign of her.

Hallett had gone out himself, in the gleaming black buggy, for he took it as a personal affront that Salvation, the town he owned, could dare to hold any secret from him. Three times that night he drove past Renton House, oblivious to the old man who rocked back and forth on the porch — old, arthritic, ineffectual Pete Nabor who had made Juanita disappear right under the sheriff's hawkish nose.

Pete had been a keen observer to the happenings all that late afternoon — the roundup of the half-senile jury, the transportation of first the girl to the church, then the big stranger — and when he'd seen her running frenziedly into Sinai Street, obviously with no idea which way to turn, he had waved to her, called out for her to come to the porch.

And something in the tone of his voice had reached the girl's intuition, persuaded her against anything that was purely reasonable that he wanted to help. So she came to him, and in half-forgotten pidgin-Spanish he showed her the little doorway in the side of the staircase that opened onto a surprisingly spacious stone-walled room. Nabor knew about its existence for the simple reason that he had built this hotel twenty years ago, when all this country had been known as the San Joaquin Strip. He'd been one of the first mountain men to come down and trade with the Mexicans. Now it was Salvation, and the Mexicans had been driven out, but there were still a few things about it that Sidney Hallett would have to learn for himself.

The hours dragged by, the fruitless search was repeated over and over again, and Juanita, of course, stayed safe and snug in her hideout. Nabor kept up a running conversation with her, enjoying to the hilt this measure of satisfaction against the sheriff he so cordially hated. He even managed to smuggle down the supper of ham and beans that the maid served to him on the porch. The girl told him of Hallett's treachery, voiced her concern that she had somehow been instrumental in a plot against *El Fuerte* — Buchanan.

The old man's reassurance on that was almost an echo of what Buchanan himself had told Ellen Booth.

"He's in a fix," Nabor admitted. "No doubt of that. But they ain't hung him yet."

The night wore on, hot and sultry, and despite his assurances to Hallett that the Mexican was not on River Street, Bull Hynman returned there, took up a place at the end of Birdy Warren's bar and by his surly presence put a damper on any revelry that evening. He ordered a private bottle and began to drink from it. Though the liquor made no visible change in his outward appearance it began to slowly channel his uncomplicated mind into another channel. He told himself again that this was, after all, his night off from duty. The escape of the little Mex had Hallett all worked up, but Bull Hynman, for one, couldn't get that excited about it.

Oh, a nice-lookin' piece and all that, he grunted, what with her dark features and girlish young figure. But she was to hell and gone tonight, and like the fella once said, a bird in the hand. The fella also said, Bull reminded himself, that they're all alike when the light is out — and that was no farther away than crossing River Street to Maude's. He was treated real good over there, and not just because he belted the tarts around every so often to keep 'em in line. He was treated good because, god dammit, he was Chief Deputy Sheriff, the second from the top and a man of importance. Hell, he was doin' 'em a favor and they were grateful. That was it, grateful.

All except the damn little Mex, and she didn't know any better. *And all except Ellen Booth,* he suddenly thought. She knew better — knew damn well better that Bull Hynman was someone who counted for something. *And her married to a sneakin' little thief and puttin' on airs!* Hynman drained his glass of raw whisky.

The impulse to cross the street to Maude's was gone. In its place was born the picture of the blonde and ripe-bodied young woman languishing all alone in the night in the jail cell. Well, all alone except for the drifter — and with the dawn there'd be an end to him.

He corked the bottle, pushed himself away from the bar and strode from the place. No bill had been presented, no payment offered, and the distraught Birdy was just as happy to leave it at that in exchange for his departure.

Hynman came back to Sinai Street, observed by no one but the ever-vigilant Pete Nabor. He found Enos dozing noisily at Hallett's desk. He knocked the man's boots from their comfortable position and Enos came awake with a jerk.

"What?" he asked. "What'sa matter?"

"Get up and go home," Hynman growled at him. "I'm takin' your trick."

Enos blinked. It was not like the straw boss to offer any favors.

"I do somethin' wrong?" he asked.

"Sleepin' on the job. Now get on out of here. And don't forget there's a hangin' tomorrow mornin'."

"I'll be here," Enos said, shuffling sleepily around the desk and on out into the night. Hynman waited a moment, then went to the street door and slid home the bolt. He crossed to the connecting door, a candle in one hand, the bottle in the other, and thumbed it open, stepped inside and pulled it closed with the heel of his boot. He moved across the room. In the one cell was Buchanan, sprawled face down on the cot with his wrists still tied, just as they had left him. His breathing was even, heavy with sleep.

He gazed into the other cell, holding the candle at arm's length. She slept, too, on her back, and his eyes fastened on the skirt of her thin cotton dress, where it had become hiked above her knee.

They were not all alike when the light is out, he thought excitedly. Suddenly she stirred and Hynman extinguished the candle.

"Is someone there?" Ellen's voice asked in the dark.

Hynman set the candle on the floor, reached

into his pocket for the key.

"Who is it?" Ellen asked. "Who is there?"

He fitted the key into the lock, turned it and opened the door.

"Get out of here!" she cried. "Get out —"

He fell on her, his rough hand clamped over her mouth. She twisted beneath him, violently, and the bottle of whisky he held in his other hand crashed to the stone floor and broke into a hundred fragments.

"God damn you, anyhow!" Hynman snarled, plunged into a blind rage by the fierceness of her resistance. She tried to roll out from under him, to claw at his face, to bring her knees up — tried so many ways to defend herself that she was exhausting her strength completely. And he seemed to know what he was about, kept pressing his two-hundred pounds down on her, wearing her out. Out of pure terror the girl found a reserve to stave off the man's lust and she swung them both from the narrow cot. In an instant she was on her feet, backing away from him, but Hynman was as aware as Ellen was of the open cell door and he spread his arms wide, boxed her into a corner. He moved in on her slowly, relentlessly, and when his hands descended on her shoulders all her resistance to fight him deserted her.

Hynman swung her around, started to bear her back to the cot. Then all at once he gave a strangling sound and the fight went out of him. Buchanan had him, had the man's neck locked good in the crook of his arm, and Hynman's frantic

121

gurgling was about as sweet to his ears as anything he could ever recall hearing. A piece of the jagged glass had served to free his hands, after being awakened by the girl's outcry, and now he was enjoying himself completely.

It was happening much too fast for Ellen Booth to comprehend all that was going on. But one thing she knew just by the sound of it — a man was being killed in the dark — and she didn't want that to happen on her account.

"Stop," she called to Buchanan. "Stop before it's too late."

"He knows he's got this coming," Buchanan answered matter-of-factly.

"Please," she said. "Please don't kill him."

Buchanan sighed, released the pressure slightly. With his free hand he reached into Hynman's pocket, removed the key, then slid the other man's Colt from its holster and hefted it fondly. "Pleasant dreams," he told the deputy and cracked the butt just once behind his ear. Hynman slid down the bars, unconscious, and Buchanan stuck the gun in his waistband, unlocked the cell and let himself out of jail.

"Well, come on," he said to Ellen.

"You mean — just walk out of here?"

"Not unless you like the service you're getting. Come on."

"But that *would* be breaking a law," she said and Buchanan gave a laugh that mirrored his wonder at a woman's point of view.

"Far be it from me," he told her, "to start

122

you on a life of crime. Recommend, though, that you lock yourself away from bruiser-boy." He stepped into her cell, reached out with the key. Their hands brushed and suddenly the girl's slim fingers took hold of his wrist.

"I'll come along," she murmured, still clinging to him as he led the way out. It was midnight. Salvation slept. So far as Buchanan could see along dark Sinai Street there was no one else about but the two of them.

"Now let's really break the law," he suggested.

"What?"

"We're going to borrow the deputy's pony," he said, unhitching Hynman's horse from the rail and swinging into the saddle. "Reach up," he told Ellen then, and when she gave him her hand he swung her effortlessly up behind him, turned the mount in the direction of River Street.

"Where can I take you?" he asked.

"I don't know," she said worriedly. "There's no place to go."

"My own horse is in the livery," he said. "You're welcome to ride along to Sacramento."

"Sacramento? You mean — just the two of us?"

"Invite anybody else you want to . . ."

"Psst! You there — big fella! Come over here!" The low, urgent-sounding voice came from the direction of the hotel.

"Who are you?" Buchanan called back.

"A friend, dangit! Come here!"

"It's Pete Nabor," Ellen said. "Let's see what he wants."

Buchanan edged in toward the building, in no particular mood to chew the fat with Pete Nabor or any other citizen of Salvation.

"So ye broke out, did ye?" the old man greeted him gleefully. "Knew ye would — just knew it!"

"Anything else you wanted?"

"Did ye stop Hynman's clock fer 'em?" Nabor asked in high expectation.

"No," Buchanan said, his own voice regretful. "Well, got to push along, Captain," he said, swinging the horse.

"Not so dang fast, sonny. You're takin' another passenger, wherever you're goin'."

"You can't come, Pete," Ellen Booth put in.

"Not me. Juanita."

"Juanita? They didn't stick her back in that crib?"

"She's right under these stairs, sleepin' like a babe."

Buchanan dismounted.

"Jest swing the third step outward," Nabor instructed, and sure enough it was a door on hinges. Buchanan stuck his head and shoulders through.

"Muchacha," he called. "Wake up!"

"El Fuerte!" came the answer a moment later. "I knew you would come for me!"

Folks seemed to know a lot more than he did, Buchanan reflected, and then the girl was directly in front of him. He backed out of the opening and she followed.

"Up you go," he told her, boosting her into the saddle. The dark-haired girl looked around

124

at the blonde one and Juanita spoke a greeting.

"What did she say?" Ellen asked.

"Now, wait," Buchanan said firmly. "We're not going through that business again." He went forward, picked the reins over the horse's head. "So long," he said to Pete Nabor and started off along the street.

"Take care of yeselves," Nabor called after them. *"Vaya con Dios,"* he added for Juanita, and with his voice still echoing in the warm night air the thing happened.

Lafe Jenkins, the cautious one, took two brief steps from the shadows and opened fire without a word of warning. A hot slug slammed into Buchanan's shoulder, spinning him halfway around and down to one knee. Two more shots screamed past his head. He whipped Hynman's unfamiliar gun from his trouser tops and the hammer fell with a sickening click on an empty chamber. He triggered again and a live bullet roared toward the muzzle flash of Jenkins' .45. He hit him with a second shot, a third, and then there was no target as Lafe lay sprawled and unmoving in the dust of Sinai Street.

The girls astride the horse had been struck dumb by the suddenness of the attack, the terrifying din. Ellen Booth stared almost sightlessly at the gunsmoke curling lazily upward. She was brought slowly back to her surroundings by the acrid smell of gunpowder in her nostrils.

"How awful," she said in a wavering voice. "How awful." The other one began to cry very softly — and a moment later both fell silent, aware almost simultaneously that there was neither sound nor movement from Buchanan. The man still knelt on one knee, his hand pressed to his bullet-torn shoulder, his head bowed tiredly. His attitude seemed to say that there is some limit to human endurance.

Ellen Booth was beside him in an instant. Juanita followed.

"What can I do for you?" Ellen asked. "How can I help you?"

Lights were being lit in the various houses. Faces appeared in open windows.

"Ride out of here," Buchanan told her. "Hallett will be coming."

"No," Ellen said. "No." She put her arm around his back, another beneath his arm. "Try to stand," she told him. "Lean on me." Juanita gave her support to the other side, and together, plus the big man's effort, they got him erect. "Walk," Ellen said. "Just a few steps." She guided him to the stirrup and both girls lifted his boot to it. Then, working together, they had him in the saddle. Ellen went quickly to gather up the reins again, motioned to the other girl. "Come on," she said and they started off for River Street a second time.

Chapter Ten

I'm awake," Buchanan said.

"I know," Ellen Booth told him. "I heard a change in your breathing."

"And wherever I am, it feels awful good."

"You're at the ranch," she said. "This used to be my father's room."

Buchanan, lying almost in state atop a great fourposter bed, looked around at his new surroundings with a knowing eye. There was obvious neglect here, a lack of human habitation, but those beams above his head were solid oak, that door was hung by a craftsman, the window frames were meant to last a lifetime and then some.

"How could you leave this to live in that town?" he asked mildly.

"Frank and I meant to work the place," she said. "Then he got into his trouble. I couldn't very well live here all alone."

"Guess not," he agreed, and then his face changed as he made a discovery. "What, ah, happened to my duds?" he asked.

"We washed them, Juanita and I. They're out in the sun drying."

"Real thoughtful."

"Later on we're going to wash you, too," she

informed him. "Give you a shave and cut your hair."

Buchanan cocked his head at her, ran a hand over his stubbled chin. "Guess I can manage that," he said.

"You're going to take it easy," Ellen said. "How does your shoulder feel this morning?"

"A little stiff," he lied. The wound was hurting like hell. He looked down at the bandage, grinned self-consciously. "Pretty fancy fixings," he said.

"From one of Juanita's petticoats."

"What's Juanita doing now?"

"She found some cans of things in the larder. I guess we're going to have a stew."

"Well that's fine," he said. "That's dandy. Now — how in the world did you get me up here?"

Ellen smiled. "It's funny what you do when you have to," she said. "Even two helpless females who can't understand a word of the other's. What we did was get your horse at the stable — and what a temper that animal has!"

"High spirits, mostly."

"Well, if Doc Allen hadn't gentled her, drunk as he was, we'd have never gotten you onto her back. But after that she was all right, except for biting Hynman's horse whenever he got too close."

Buchanan laughed. "Particular who she travels with," he said.

"Well, we got you here, that's the main thing. How long we can stay is another."

Then Buchanan reminded himself that this was

just another postponement after all, another delay. His mind went back to the night before, to the burning hole in his shoulder, and the inclination to just stay right there in the middle of their damn street and settle the argument once and for all. But the girls had pulled his bacon out of that fire, and if his responsibility for them had only been casual then, now it was real.

"Any weapons at all around the place?"

"Dad has a gun locker in the attic. None of them are very new — and of course Frank never owned a gun at all."

"For a fact?"

"He's city-bred," she told him. "Went to college. He didn't have to make his way with a gun. I'm sorry, Buchanan. I didn't mean that exactly like it sounded."

"I envy your husband," Buchanan said. "Suit me fine if every man in the country chucked his gun in the well and we started off brand new."

"What would you do with yourself — starting off brand new?"

"Well," he grinned, "first off I'd hunt me up a pretty girl who owned a little spread like this one. Then I'd work her skinny so's there'd always be enough for me to paint the town Saturday night."

Ellen laughed with him. "You know ranching?"

"Born and raised on one."

"Why'd you give it up?"

"The old man got wiped out, back in forty-six."

"Drought?"

Buchanan looked at the blonde, shook his head slowly.

"The land never let us down around Alpine," he said with a note of reminiscence in his deep voice. "Grass grow over your boot-tips if you give it half the chance. Just sink a pole and you got water."

"Then what happened to your ranch?"

"Couple of jaspers rode into town one Monday morning. Bearded gents. The old man and a friend of his caught up with them, but that was a year later and there wasn't a dime left of the fifty thousand."

"The fifty thousand?"

"What they stole from the Alpine Bank," Buchanan said. "Two riffraff thieves, and they wiped out a dozen men whose boots they weren't fit to lick."

"I'm sorry," Ellen said. She looked stricken.

"And so am I for telling the story," he said. "I just hope that Sheriff Hallett's made another bad guess so far as your man is concerned."

Her eyes bored into his own. "You sound skeptical," she said. "As if you think Hallett is right."

"No I don't," he said lightly. "The man who put his rope over you wouldn't rob a bank."

"Frank stands convicted of embezzlement," she said stonily.

"Well, look at me," Buchanan said, trying to banter the girl out of her mood. "I'm in the book, too. Took unfair advantage of Juanita, from the little I heard of it." He put his hand to his neck. "This should've been stretched a little a few hours ago," he said, "if you believe everything you hear."

"No," Ellen said. "There was evidence against Frank. A U.S. Marshal traveled all the way down here from San Francisco. There was — a woman involved."

"What'd your man say?"

She looked down at the bare floor. "Frank said he didn't do it. He swore that he was innocent."

"Well?"

"But the evidence! A marshal. What the woman swore on her deathbed. Frank's ring."

Just hearing it, hearing the conviction in her own voice, was enough to convince Buchanan that there had been justice done in this particular case. Now he was doubly sorry for having revived her memories. He was relieved when Juanita walked into the room.

"*Tú desperatas!*" she cried.

"*Sí,*" Buchanan said, guardedly. For this was a well-brought up señorita, and she didn't use the familiar '*tú*' lightly. In the course of nursing him, taking his clothes to wash, they had apparently entered into a rather friendly relationship — if that was the word for it.

"*Tú fuiste asi valiente!*" she said, sitting impudently on the bed. "*Asi soccorrente!*"

"What did she say?" Ellen asked.

"She thinks I have been brave — and now I look very helpless," Buchanan answered. Then he asked Juanita sternly: "*¿Donde está mi ropas?*"

131

"What did you say?" Ellen asked.

"I want to know where my duds are, that's what."

"Well you don't have to be so gruff about it."

"Better let me handle this," he said.

"Handle what?"

"The little change in relationships here," he said with a glance at the nearby Juanita. "She's starting to forget who she is."

Ellen's face turned angry. "Juanita's every bit as good as anybody I ever met," she said. "Better than most."

"Right," Buchanan agreed. "And I bet her folks are first-class people. Most likely got a fine marriage arranged for her. That's what she's got to remember."

"I'm sorry," Ellen said, gazing at Buchanan with a curious expression. "I seem to keep making mistakes about you."

"*¿Qué pasa, querido?*" Juanita asked. "Are you angry with me?"

"I'm ashamed for you," he told her. "And I am not *querido* or anything like that."

"You don't like me?"

"We are good friends, you and I," Buchanan said. "And I would also like to be your father's good friend. A friend to all your family."

"Then I shall call you *tío,*" the girl said, her pretty mouth pouting. "You are my uncle."

"Fine," Buchanan said. "And now, *sobrina mio,* please fetch my clothes in here."

She flashed the smiling man a hurt look, got

132

up from the bed and left the room.

"Did you get things settled?" Ellen asked.

"I hope so," he said. "She's my niece now."

"And that's how you want it to be?"

"That's how it *has* to be."

"Juanita isn't attractive to you at all?"

Buchanan frowned across the room at her. "Don't keep on making mistakes about me, Mrs. Booth," he said in a voice she hadn't heard before. "I'm a natural man. As natural as any man you ever stood in front of."

Her questions had been put almost flippantly; she had spoken to him from the protection of her status as a married woman. But she realized now that she had crossed over into dangerous ground, passed some invisible line that separated their worlds, for he had demolished her 'protection' with just the expression in his eyes. Now she 'stood in front of him' as a woman — and not in three manless, love-starved years had she ever felt more like one.

"Don't you speak like that to me," she said. "Don't you dare." But the words carried no conviction, had a sound of artifice even to her own ears. Ellen had enough frankness with herself — having lived so long alone — to admit that she had spoken what was expected of her, not what she wanted to tell him.

"Somebody better have a look at that stew," Buchanan said.

Ellen nodded distractedly, all but fled from the bedroom. Then Juanita came in, bearing his clothes. She dropped them in a pile at the foot of the bed, left the room and returned almost immediately with a basin of steaming-hot water, a cake of yellow soap and a bone-handled razor.

"It's been decided, then, that I need a shave?" Buchanan asked.

"Yes, Uncle," she told him, just as formally.

"Praise God for women," he said. "What a world this would be without them."

"Yes, Uncle."

"You'll have a man of your own to manage someday soon," he said to her. *"Un hombre muy guapo."*

"Who cares if he is handsome?" she said to that. "I'll spit on him."

"What kind of way is that to talk?"

"I have decided to go with the sisters," she said. "I forsake all men forever."

"You?" he said. *"¿La belleza de Salinas?"*

"I am not the beauty of Salinas," she said scornfully. "You have not looked upon Maria del Torres. I vow you would not be *El Tío* with Maria del Torres."

"I would be as a brother to Maria," Buchanan said. "Now go help Elena with the stew," he told her. "Not too much salt."

Then he had the room to himself. After the chore of shaving with a dulled blade he dressed himself and joined them in the huge kitchen.

"Say, that smells good," he commented cheerfully but his female companions ignored him, kept their backs turned. He said it again in Spanish,

134

but Juanita had suddenly developed deafness. The meal was served in silence, eaten in silence.

"Anything you two ladies want to say to each other?" Buchanan offered. "Be glad to pass it back and forth. *¿Quiere usted hablar a Elena?*" he repeated. There were no takers, and he pushed his chair away from the table with a sigh, stood up. "Mind if I take a look around your place?" he asked Ellen. She shook her head slightly and he turned to walk out. Suddenly both girls called to him, anxiously.

"You're not going away?" Ellen said.

"*¿Cuándo volvera ud?*" Juanita said.

"I wouldn't run out on you," Buchanan said. "But you both might consider going along with me to Sacramento. Ellen, you could go over to San Francisco from there, and I could put Juanita on a direct stage to Salinas."

"When would we leave?"

"Maybe tomorrow, if this shoulder's well enough to ride with."

"*¿Qué dice ud?*" Juanita asked.

"I said that tomorrow we'll start you on your way home. How will that be?"

"Good," she said. "I suppose."

Buchanan went out of the house, stood under the eaves for several minutes surveying the layout. It had apparently been a very modest spread, unpretentious. The bunkhouse with its sagging roof would sleep no more than a crew of six. There wasn't a thing his eye lit on that didn't need either to be repaired or scrapped altogether.

135

But a man wouldn't have to kill himself putting it back in operation, not if ranching was in his blood. Buchanan couldn't figure how Ellen's husband would rather spend his time stealing from a bank when he had this life handed to him on a tray. From that he found himself speculating about Frank Booth in general, wondering what the man looked like, how he talked, what it was about him that had set him heads and shoulders above the other men who must have been courting the good-looking blonde girl.

He was strolling along with his thoughts when he spied the two horses, unsaddled and grazing in the corral. The area was overgrown, sorry-looking, and he saw one section in particular where the animals were free to escape if they had a mind to. He went to it and replaced the bars that had fallen from their rungs, at the same time running a critical glance over the mustang whose lameness had been the innocent cause of his getting involved in all of Salvation's troubles. She looked fine to him, rested, and when she moved about there was no trace of a limp.

Little girl, he thought, *don't get used to the soft life. It's back to work for you tomorrow.*

He moved on beyond the corral, along the nearest thing that resembled a path from the house, and observed that this was going to be another cloudless, blistering day. The land, as he crossed it in wandering fashion, was becoming more and more wild. Up ahead there was a particularly dense growth of foliage, almost a wall. He came to it and went on through, parting the heavy shrub with his hands. It was marvelously cool in here, shaded, and on beyond the land suddenly dipped down. When Buchanan reached that point he was staring down into the greenest, clearest, most inviting little spring he had ever seen. It was oval in shape, not more than twenty feet at its widest. He let himself down the gently sloping bank to its edge. The water was crystal clean, deliciously cold. He scooped out a brimming hatful and let it cascade over his hair and shoulders. He felt like a kid again, as if he had made a discovery, and with the air of a man staking out a claim he worked his way around to the far side, where the growth was nearly tropical in its thickness and the grass reached to his knees. Obeying an impulse, Buchanan shed his clothes, his boots, slipped into the water and began floating luxuriantly in the wonderful stuff.

Had Frank Booth known about this and forsaken it? That just couldn't be possible.

He bathed in the natural pool for a good hour, then climbed out and stretched his long body flat in the long grass — one human being who was completely satisfied with life at the moment. Even his multitude of aches and pains seemed to have taken a holiday, and soon he was fast asleep.

Buchanan awoke again to the sound of voices, high-spirited female voices. He turned his head warily to the source of the happiness, peered out through the tightly clustered blades of grass. His two friends were there in the spring, having as grand a time as he had and just as naked. Ellen was standing on a ledge beneath the surface, the water lapping gently at her hips, and a thousand droplets glistened on her fair body like so many tiny diamonds. Juanita was diving beneath the surface, and whenever her head and olive-tinted shoulders reappeared Ellen splashed water at her and they both laughed uproariously. There was no strangeness between them now, no language barrier to keep them from enjoying this interlude.

And poor Buchanan — who had never rhymed two lines, never sketched so much as a cactus bush — how he yearned to be able to set down his thoughts in the grand manner, to commit that idyll to a fullblown canvas in all its golden tones. Even the water looked greener, purer, for their presence in it.

Then he came down from the clouds with a jolt. *What in the name of hell was he going to do?* He surely couldn't speak to them, call any attention to his presence at this private scene. Their embarrassment would go deep, wipe out all the lighthearted pleasure of the romp they were having. *Steal away then?* He looked up the slope of the bank, at the prickly obstacles in his path near the top, the place where the growth was not so thick. A man his size, encumbered by two gunshot wounds plus duds and boots couldn't count on exiting anyplace unnoticed.

But what you can damn well do is give them their privacy, he told himself severely, promptly rolling over on his back again and gazing at the blue sky overhead. The decision, then, was to stay put right where he was — a fine one, for he could still fill his ears with their happy sounds and not be an intruder.

The girls splashed and cavorted for another thirty minutes, then an exhausted kind of quiet settled over the place.

"He's probably starved for dinner," Ellen said, her voice floating across the water to Buchanan's hearing. "We'd better go feed him."

"No comprende ud." Juanita said.

"The man," Ellen said. "What do you call him — *El Tío?*"

"Oh, sí. El Tío," Juanita said, and her voice broke in a burst of laughter that was discomfiting to the eavesdropper on the far bank. Then, to make it worse, Ellen joined in the mirth.

"I know, Juanita," she said, giggling. "I know what you mean. Whatever he is, he's no proper uncle. He's *no tío,*" she repeated and that sent Juanita into a fresh spasm.

The man suffered their levity with a scowl, wondering what was so funny. Then his own good humor reasserted itself and he smiled at the image he saw of himself as the uncle of a high-born Mexican young lady. He heard them leave the pool then, and when the silence was absolute fifteen minutes later he ventured another peek through the foliage and found them gone. With that he dressed himself, started back toward the ranch house by a circuitous route.

139

He found them busy as two bees in the kitchen, their faces shining, their still-damp hair piled atop their heads. Despite what he thought was the gallant attitude to take, Buchanan could not help picturing them as they had been.

"Stew again," Ellen informed him.

"Fine."

"What did you do with yourself all afternoon?"

"Took a siesta."

"Juanita and I had some real fun. We went swimming."

"That's nice."

She grinned up at him, her eyes dancing with harmless flirtation. "I know something you don't," she said teasingly.

"What's that?"

"Your pretty niece is not a little girl."

Buchanan almost nodded his agreement with that, was saved by Juanita's own voice that made him turn his head.

"What does Elena say to you?" she asked.

"That you are a fine swimmer. And that you are a fine cook if you will not put too much salt in the stew," he said in Spanish.

"That is what she says?"

"The salt is what I say."

Their second meal together was more of a social success, with both girls keeping Buchanan very active translating. They wanted to know more about each other, and Juanita's particular interest was in Ellen's husband. What did he look like, how old was he, and *where* was he?

Ellen, so candid about him previously, hedged on Frank Booth's whereabouts. She asked Buchanan to explain that he was away on a business trip, that she was going to meet him in San Francisco. As for his physical appearance, she described a man of medium height, slender, with curly black hair and a smiling face. He was twenty-seven years old.

Then Ellen wanted to hear about Juanita's home in Salinas, what she was taught at the mission school, and was properly sympathetic to learn that the other girl's father was ill.

Buchanan finally called a halt, protesting good-naturedly that he'd had to talk more in the past hour than in all his previous lifetime.

"And your shoulder hurts, too, doesn't it?" Ellen asked.

"Some," he admitted.

"Let me change the bandage," she said but he shook his head, rose from the table.

"It'll be all right," he assured her, but he was holding his left side stiffly, and when he turned and left the room a small frown appeared between his eyes. It was not that the wound was any more painful than it had been, but now there was a burning sensation beneath the bandage. He wondered if the damn thing hadn't become infected.

If that were the case, a helluva lot of help he'd be to old Jack Maguire and his railroad.

He took his trouble on out of the house, walking in a different direction than before, hoping to see enough things of interest to make him forget the shoulder. But the open range has little variety — and this was open country with not another sign of human habitation for as far as the eye could see. The sun was setting as he started back, the air became muggy, and the dampness made him feel still more uncomfortable.

When he came back into the house again it was dark outside. The girls were sitting placidly in the parlor, a lamp shedding its comfortable light on their faces.

"It's worse, isn't it?" Ellen asked knowingly.

"They act up in the night," Buchanan told her. "It'll be all right by morning."

"You're sure you don't want the bandage changed?"

"I'm sure, thanks."

"What time did you want to get started to-morrow?"

"Sunup, if possible. Can't push my bronc too hard for a while yet, so it'll be an all-day trip."

She nodded and stood up. "In that case I think I'll go to bed now. How do you say good night in Spanish?"

"Buenas noches."

She repeated it to Juanita with a kind of proud little smile.

"Dice usted 'good night'," Buchanan told the Mexican and when she said the words she also smiled.

"There you go," he said. "Pretty soon you'll be chattering away like magpies." He waved to them, walked off down the hallway to the bedroom he was using.

Sleep came hard and slow. For the next two hours he lay on his back, dozing occasionally, coming sharply awake with the continuous throbbing ache. About midnight he found himself sitting up in bed and staring feverishly at Ellen Booth. She stood beside him in a cotton chemise, a candle in her hand, its flame revealing the deep concern in her face.

"What's the matter?" Buchanan asked.

"You groaned terribly," she said. "Don't you remember?"

He shook his head. "Sorry I woke you."

"Wait a minute," she said suddenly. "I think I remember the place." With that she left the room, and when she came back she held a bottle of 100-proof whisky in her hand. "I would have poured this on last night," she explained, "but I couldn't think where my father kept it."

Buchanan eyed the bottle dubiously as he peeled off his shirt.

"Seems pretty wasteful . . ."

"Nonsense. But maybe you'd better take a good drink of it first." She handed him the bottle and he uncorked it, took a pull in direct ratio to his size. Ellen looked a little startled when he returned the bottle.

"Now lie down," she told him, and when he was prone she took off the bandage. "It's all red," she said worriedly. "It's going to hurt something fierce when the whisky touches it."

"Can't be helped."

She poured the straight liquor directly onto the wound and Buchanan's whole enormous frame went taut with the shocking pain of it. His eyes shut tight, and the two large tendons alongside his neck were stretched so tight that Ellen thought they would snap.

"Oh, dear God!" she cried out, throwing herself across his chest fitfully, as if somehow she could shield him with her own body, absorb some of his suffering.

Neither of them were aware that another presence had come into the room, a man who stood in the doorway with a look of murderous rage in his too-handsome face.

"HARLOT!" he shouted, and at the terrible sound Ellen's head swung around.

"Frank — !"

"Stand away from him, you cheating, two-faced jezebel!"

"Frank, Frank — you don't understand —"

"I have eyes! Stand away —"

Now she saw the gun in his hand and she got to her feet, stood squarely between her husband and the man on the bed. The raw alcohol was still searing Buchanan's festering wound and he was only half-aware of what else was happening.

"He was shot, Frank," Ellen was pleading. "Helping me. There's nothing between us. I swear to you —"

Then, from down the hall, Juanita's piercing scream filled the house.

That aroused Buchanan, brought him erect.

Frank Booth made a half-turn, seemed frozen with indecision.

"Juanita — what is it!" Ellen called to her in a voice on the thin edge of hysteria. Buchanan brushed past her, shouldered Booth out of his way as he stalked down the hallway.

"*No me toca!*" Juanita was crying to someone.

"*Tenga calma!*" a rough voice told her.

Buchanan stepped into the room, came up behind another big man and pulled him around. "Take it easy yourself, brother," he told him raggedly. "Come on out of here."

"Hands off!" the intruder growled, but when he tried to jerk his arm free the grip only tightened and he found himself out in the black hallway a moment later. Buchanan let go of him then.

"Luth — what the hell's going on down there?" Frank Booth called.

"How do I know? This your ranch, or ain't it?"

Booth had the candle in his hand, came toward them. The light flickered brightly on what looked like a brand new Colt in his hand. He had to raise the candle to peer into Buchanan's face, then his glance took in the gunwound in his shoulder, the bandage at his ribs.

"Who're you?" he demanded.

"The name's Buchanan."

"What're you doing in my house?"

Buchanan laughed wryly. "Resting up for a trip tomorrow morning," he said.

"How come you pick my place?"

"Frank," Ellen interrupted, "you don't understand what's been happening down in Salvation. Buchanan helped me."

"Yeah? How?"

"Sheriff Hallett was holding me in jail. He said I was a hostage to make sure you wouldn't make trouble."

"The dirty sonofabitch!"

"Frank!"

Her husband looked at her in surprise. Then a crooked smile crossed his face. "I'm changed some, Ellen," he said. "I don't sing in the choir anymore."

"And you carry a gun," she said. "What is that for?"

"To protect myself, that's what for. I'm all through being pushed around by the goddam Sid Halletts." He said it defiantly, but Buchanan observed that he didn't want to return his wife's steady gaze. Instead, he swung to the tall man. "If you helped Ellen, I'm obliged," he said. "But you can do your sleeping out in the bunkhouse."

"Frank, he's wounded! See for yourself."

"The bunkhouse is fine with me," Buchanan said quietly. "So long as he bunks there, too," he added, nodding at the other one.

"I'm company, friend. I sleep right here."

"Your name is Luther Reeves?"

"That's right — and what's it to you?"

"We'll bunk together," Buchanan told him.

Reeves was nearly as tall as Buchanan but his body was stringier, slack-looking, and his face had a hungry, furtive expression. Now he was plainly measuring the man opposite with his thin-spaced appraising eyes.

"The bunkhouse ain't my style," he said thinly, apparently deciding that the gun at his hip was the big difference between them.

"I think you'd better," Ellen said then. "There's a young girl here . . ."

"And what of it?"

"We know who you are, Mr. Reeves," she said. "We know all about your fine record."

At that, Reeves glanced sharply to Frank Booth.

"You had everything all fixed," he said accusingly.

"Something went wrong, dammit," Booth answered, then turned on Ellen. "What'd you do, run to Hallett with my letter?"

She didn't answer for a long moment.

"Well?"

"You know I wouldn't do a thing like that, Frank," she told him, a tone of disillusion in her voice. "Hallett intercepted your letter — and he already had information on this man. What are you doing with such a person, anyhow?"

"Ah, don't you believe them stories about me," Reeves said. "I never did nobody any harm."

"How about the woman you raped?"

"*Raped? Me?* Why, you never heard such a trumped-up charge. That girl was ready, willing and able . . ."

"Come on, Reeves," Buchanan said wearily. "I got some sleeping to do tonight."

"Then go, for crissake, and get it!" the man snarled, switching without effort from the wheedling voice he had just been using. Suddenly he had his back hard against the wall, with Buchanan's thumb and forefinger imprisoning his neck pitchfork style.

"Mister, I'm as tender as a boil tonight," Buchanan told him. "On top of that I took a gut-whacking yesterday on your account. What you want to do is oblige me by marching to hell out of here toward that bunkhouse."

Reeves had both hands free and he knew that all he had to do was draw either gun on his hip. But the more he stared into this wild man's face the less inclined he was to show him who was boss. Frank Booth broke the silence.

"Maybe you better, Luth," he said. "We'll get this thing all straightened out tomorrow."

"Let's go," Buchanan said, without Booth's deference, and pushed Reeves ahead of him, crowded him along the hall toward the front door. "Thanks for the treatment, Ellen," he called back through the darkness. "I think it helped."

"I'm glad," she said. "Good night."

" 'Night." He opened the door, moved the still-reluctant Reeves on through, closed it behind them. "The bunkhouse is over this way," he said.

"What's your game, anyhow? What're you proddin' me for?"

"So I can get to sleep."

They reached the dilapidated building and Bu-

148

chanan had to force the door ajar on its squeaking hinges.

"Home sweet home," Reeves complained, going inside unwillingly. "Christ, what a hole."

"Turn around, Luther."

"What?"

Buchanan turned him, deftly unbuckled the man's gunbelt.

"What the hell you think you're *doin'?*"

"You don't sleep with 'em, do you?"

"None of your business what I do with 'em."

Buchanan laughed in his face. "Luther," he said, "if I ever had any business it's your hardware. Now go pick yourself a feather bed and get to sleep."

"How do I know you won't plug me?"

"Now you're putting ideas into my head. Just go bunk down, will you? And sleep?"

Reeves made an indignant sound, muttered an obscenity. But he was moving away all the same, abandoning his guns to Buchanan's care and searching out a bunk. Buchanan's own choice was the cot nearest the door, but first he tossed the desperado's gunbelt out of the building, then swung the cot directly across the doorway. If Reeves wanted his weapons he would have to get by Buchanan — if he wanted them that much.

"Sleep tight, Luther," Buchanan advised him.

"Ah, go to hell," his roommate answered with a growl.

Chapter Eleven

In the main house there was also mistrust and strain, and Ellen Booth was a young woman with badly mixed emotions. On the one hand she was grateful to have her husband free again — but she couldn't put out of her mind that the first word she'd heard from his lips in three years was *harlot,* that he had jumped immediately to the worst conclusion about her. And there was the gun in his hand, the certainty she had that if there hadn't been the other interruption he would surely have fired it at the defenseless, unarmed Buchanan — that he might even have killed her. Ellen was also deeply disturbed by the other change in him, the hard tone of voice, the barroom language, the snarling defiance of the law. Most worrisome of all was the obvious bond between her husband and this Luther Reeves. Frank had thrown in with the man, they were partners, and what chilled her very heart was the fear of what business that partnership was engaged in.

So now, as he followed her into the bedroom, she felt as if she were alone with a stranger, as if she had been thrust into an intimate situation against her will. Ellen was actually embarrassed to stand before him in her underclothes, and it came to her as a kind of shock that she would be more at ease with the real stranger, Buchanan. Even more than that — she missed his presence in the house.

"Don't shut the door, Frank," she said.

"Why not?"

"And please blow out the candle."

"I want to look at you," he said. "It's been a long time."

"Very long. Please blow out the candle."

Instead, Booth walked closer to her, bathed her naked shoulders in the yellow glow.

"It was all right for him to see," he said and Ellen bent forward angrily, extinguished the flame with a whoosh.

"Well, I'll be damned!" her husband exploded. "Grown real willful-like, haven't you?"

"I've learned to manage for myself," she said.

"And what is that supposed to mean?"

"That I won't be taken advantage of."

"*Advantage of?* You're my wife, by God — or did you forget that?"

"Not for a minute, Frank. Not for one second in three years . . ."

"Then what do you act like this for? 'Don't shut the door!' 'Blow out the candle!' Some home-coming this is!"

"It's what you made of it, Frank," she told him, keeping her own voice low.

"What was I supposed to make of it? There you are — in bed with a man! Throwing yourself all over him! I'm thinking I'm lucky I didn't walk in five minutes later —"

151

Her hand struck him across the face hard, stunned him into silence.

"That's something you shouldn't have done," he said.

"It was something you shouldn't have said," she told him.

"No one hits me," he said. "Not anyone. Not anymore."

"What is it that's changed you so?" she asked unhappily. "What happened to the Frank Booth that went away?"

"That poor damn fool?" he said contemptuously. "He's dead. Dead and buried. Sheriff Sidney Hallett killed that one. Now we're going to see how he makes out against the new Frank Booth."

"So you did come back to cause trouble — just as he said."

Booth laughed harshly. "So Mr. Holier-Than-Thou is expecting trouble, is he? Well he's sure going to get it. Right where it'll hurt him hardest."

"You plan to kill him?"

"If I get the chance I'll kill him. But if I don't it won't make too much difference. Not when his bank is cleaned out."

"I can't believe it's the same person talking," Ellen said. "The man I married —"

"I'm not the same man. You've got a better man now, a stronger one. This one knows just what he wants and how to get it. Where you going?"

The girl had stifled a sob, started to push past him in the dark. His hand gripped her bare arm, stopped her.

"I said where are you going?"

"Let me be!"

He released her arm, but his body was directly in her path, blocking. Now he took a backward step, slammed the heavy door shut.

"Open it, Frank. I don't want to be in here with you."

"I *do* want you in here."

"Against my will?" she asked him hollowly.

"You've forgotten a vow you took, wife. To love, honor *and* obey."

"A vow I'd keep — if you were the man I made it to."

" 'For better or for worse,' " Booth's voice recited, almost as if she had spoken. " 'In sickness and in health. Until death us do part . . .' "

"You said a moment ago that my Frank Booth was dead. Now I want to leave this room."

"And go where — to the bunkhouse?"

Ellen said nothing.

"Is that where you'd rather be?" Booth demanded. "Laying down in the bunkhouse?"

"Let me warn you about something, Frank," Ellen said very quietly. "That man you met here tonight — Buchanan. Don't ever let him hear you accuse him of what you accuse me."

"No? And what will he do?"

"He'll take you and he'll beat you," she promised him. "I think he'd thrash you to within one inch of your life."

"Maybe tomorrow he'll have his chance."

"But don't count on that brand new gun you bought for yourself. Lafe Jenkins' gun didn't save him."

"Jenkins?" Booth said, and there was an entirely different note in his voice. "What about Lafe Jenkins?"

"Lafe is dead. And the last I saw of the invincible Bull Hynman he was flat on his back. And Enos. You remember big, tough Enos, don't you, Frank?"

"I remember them all," Booth said sulkingly. "Who's this friend of yours supposed to be — a gunfighter?"

"A friend," Ellen said, "a man," and if she sounded proud to say it she didn't care if her husband noted it.

"But what does he do?" Booth asked. "How come he got himself tangled up with Hallett's crew?" The subject seemed very important.

"You can stop thinking about him in that way, too," Ellen said.

"What way?"

"That he'd have anything to do with you and Luther Reeves."

"How long you been carrying on with him?" Booth asked then, nastily.

"We've been having our affair since yesterday afternoon," Ellen said scornfully. "It was about two o'clock, and I was being arrested at the time. I met him later on in the afternoon, but he was busy with Mr. Hallett, and after that we were left all alone, except for some bars between us . . ."

There was a light knock on the door, then Juanita's voice from the other side, calling her name. Booth opened the door a crack, looked out at the Mexican girl's dark figure.

"What do you want?"

"*Yo quiero Elena.*"

"Speak English."

"She can't," Ellen said, moving to the door and pulling it ajar. She stepped into the hallway, put her hands on the other girls shoulders and tried to reassure her by tone of voice.

"The *hombre* is not in the house, Juanita. The bad *hombre*. Buchanan took him out of here."

Juanita nodded her head, as if she understood.

"Who's she?" Booth asked.

"Another friend," Ellen said. "He helped her, too."

"I'll bet he did."

"Don't judge all men by that Luther Reeves," Ellen told him with warmth.

"You don't know anything about Luth. He's got guts."

"Yes, I saw."

"What'd you expect him to do — start shooting right here in the house?"

"He's not in the house now, and it's still very peaceful."

"Don't you worry — old Luth'll handle that guy in his own way, in his own good time."

"I wouldn't count on it, Frank. If I were you I'd break clean with Luther Reeves. Break clean and start over." She stepped closer to him, her voice softening. "Give up these new ideas of yours," she said. "Try to forget prison and be the person you were before. I've forgiven you . . ."

"Forgiven me what?"

"The embezzling. That woman in San Francisco."

"I told you there was no embezzling, that there was no woman. Didn't you believe me?"

"Frank, I tried to believe you. I tried so hard. But all that evidence . . ."

"*All that evidence,*" he mimicked unpleasantly. "Lies! Filthy, rotten lies! Hallett worked out the whole thing!"

Ellen moved back again, let the sound of his violent protest echo and die. "I'm going to stay with Juanita," she said then.

"Stay with anyone you please!" he shouted, more furious than ever. The door closed in her face.

And so passed the night — what was left of it — in the rugged and lonely hills above Salvation.

Buchanan had the sleeping habits of a cat. Let him unwind his six-and-a-half feet someplace where there was peace, some measure of security, and the amiable giant could pass out until the hour hand came full circle. But bedded down amidst the chance of trouble, in the same room with the likes of Luther Reeves, and it was as if some sentry patrolled the corridors of his mind.

It wasn't even dawn, just the leaden grayness separating night from day, when he awoke and turned in pure reflex toward the loudly snoring Reeves. A turn of the head the other way showed Reeves' gunbelt lying in the grass where it had been thrown. He checked over his own condition then and found himself much nearer whole than he'd been twenty-four hours earlier. The whisky treatment had killed the infection, and though there was still considerable stiffness the wound had the *feel* of being better.

He left the bunkhouse then, made his way to the main building and let himself inside very quietly. His destination was the attic, and after he'd climbed up there he quickly located the gunlocker Ellen had mentioned. Her father had collected a variety of weapons, all of them rusted and risky-looking, but at the bottom of the chest, wrapped in a heavy flannel shirt, Buchanan found a Colt .45. Its workings might not be as smooth and quick to the touch as the gun Hallett had confiscated, but it certainly seemed like a piece that would give a good account of itself. He loaded it from an ample supply of ammunition, appropriated a belt and holster, and descended again. Requirement number two was food, and the larder yielded up flour for biscuits and coffee. Minutes later he had his fire going in the big stove, and not long after that his breakfast was acooking.

Buchanan was in the midst of enjoying it when he looked up to find Ellen Booth watching him from the kitchen doorway. She had found an old blouse in a bureau drawer, one she had worn before her figure had ripened, and beneath it a faded skirt from the same days of her girlhood.

"Mornin'," Buchanan greeted her, pleased to have company but a little disconcerted at the snug fit of the thin blouse. "Lead weights and mud on the menu — if you're that starved."

Ellen smiled at him, walked into the spacious room. "I'd enjoy a biscuit," she said, "if there's enough."

"That's the worst thing about them — there's plenty."

"Don't get up," she told him. "I can help my-self." She went by him to the stove, returned with two half-burned, dry-looking biscuits on a plate and a mug of the blackest coffee she'd ever seen.

"Never cooked on a stove before," Buchanan explained apologetically. "Fire got so hot it fooled me."

"These are delicious," Ellen said in kindness if not in truth.

"Well, you can always throw 'em at Hallett if he comes bothering you up here."

She didn't smile at that, only looked at him over the rim of the mug.

"You're leaving, then?"

"Soon as my niece is ready. And I'd like to buy this rig I found in the attic."

She shook her head. "You can have it," she said.

"Couldn't do that."

"I want you to."

"Well, I'll send it back from Sacramento —" Buchanan stopped, surprised by the curious expression in her face. "What's the matter?"

"I want to go with you," Ellen said. "The way we planned."

"But your husband is here," Buchanan answered, puzzled. "No point anymore in going to 'Frisco."

"He's going to rob the bank in Salvation. I'm leaving him . . ."

Frank Booth's voice broke over hers. "Now ain't this a cozy, though," he said sarcastically. "Not intruding, am I?"

Buchanan studied him for a moment. "Come on in, Booth," he told him. "Help yourself to breakfast — such as it is."

"Well, thank you. Thank you very much. Not often a man gets invited to eat at his own table with his own wife."

Buchanan looked from one to the other, frowning. Booth got his biscuits and coffee, sat down with them.

"Nice outfit you got on, Mrs. Booth," he said then. "Fine for entertaining guests."

"It's all I have, Frank," she told him. "I couldn't abide wearing my dress another day without washing it."

"Imagine you prefer this getup, anyhow —

don't you?" Booth asked Buchanan.

Buchanan set his coffee down, spoke evenly. "Any opinion I have of your wife's clothes," he said, "doesn't matter one way or the other."

Booth's caustic glance raked Ellen's face. "Is that true?" he asked her. "His opinion doesn't matter to you?"

"Frank — remember that warning I gave you last night."

"I remember it all right," he said, swinging back to Buchanan. "I've got to be real careful with you, don't I?" he asked. "You're about the toughest man-eater that ever rode the turn-pike."

Buchanan started to say one thing, changed his mind, ended up by pushing his chair away from the table and slowly rising.

"Yes, sir," Booth went on in the same tone. "I better not say what I'm thinking — even though I know it's a fact."

"Frank!"

Buchanan's big hands rested on the top of the chair. His face betrayed no emotion. "You know what to be a fact, mister?" he asked.

Booth looked up at him. "You're too damn friendly with my wife," he said, hedging now that the chips were down.

"And what's your meaning of 'friendly'?" Buchanan asked then.

"Having her nurse you. Taking breakfast together, just the two of you."

"Anything else?"

"You tell me if there's anything else," Frank Booth said.

Buchanan sighed. "I've seen men throw away their chances," he told the other man. "Everybody's entitled to make at least one mistake. But you're convincing me that you are this world's prize fool."

"Is that your answer?"

"Yeh, that's my answer," Buchanan said wearily, turning his back on him and walking away.

"Buchanan — where are you going?" Ellen called after him.

"To wake Juanita," he said. "We've got to get a move on."

"I'll wake her," Ellen offered, moving toward him quickly.

"Thanks."

"I take it you're leaving," Frank Booth said.

"That's right."

"With the Mex girl?"

"That's right."

"You got all the women you want, don't you?"

"That's right, too," Buchanan said, determined not to fight with Ellen's husband no matter what the provocation.

"Makes for an interesting life," Booth said.

"Sure does."

"But not a helluva lot of money in it."

"No," Buchanan agreed. "But what I do make is my own."

"How's that?" Booth asked sharply.

"My own, mister. I don't take what another

161

man has worked for."

"I'm taking what's owed me!" Booth shouted, getting to his feet. "I'm paying Sid Hallett back for the three long years he stole out of my life!"

Buchanan cocked his head curiously at the man's choice of words.

"Your wife says you claim to've gotten a railroading," he said.

"You're damn well told I did! I never touched a nickel of that money — but by God, he's going to pay me now!"

"Well," Buchanan said noncommittally, "this Hallett bird ain't a particular pal of mine, either. I mean, I don't figure to put him down in my will. But even if I had the grief you claim I don't think I'd plunder his bank to square it."

"How would you square it?"

"Man to man," Buchanan answered simply. "I'd ride on down into that town of his and call him out."

"*Call him out?* What chance do you think I'd have of getting to his front door?"

Buchanan was stroking his chin, looking unhappy again.

"I'm long overdue north of here," he began, "but I'll tell you what. You and me'll go down there right now and brace them. Matter of fact, he's shy a deputy at the moment . . ."

"You and me and Luther?" Booth asked, interested in the proposal. But Buchanan shook his head firmly.

"I wouldn't take help from that one if I was snake bit," he said. "What I'd do, were I you, is boot his tail on out of camp."

"Reeves is a friend of mine. We served time together."

"And that young lady inside is a wife of yours. Give her a chance and she'll serve all the rest of your time with you."

Booth brushed that aside with an impatient wave of his head. "I like your idea," he said. "I like it even better than robbing his damned bank. But I wouldn't do it without Luther . . ."

"Wouldn't do what, Frank?" Luther Reeves said, crossing the threshold of the kitchen, coming to stand quartered from Buchanan. He had his guns strapped on again, and though he'd spoken to Booth his full attention was on Buchanan — and the gun he now sported.

"Wouldn't call a showdown with this sheriff," Booth answered. "Not unless you were there to side me."

"Since when are we showdowning with any sheriff?" Reeves said. "What we been planning for two years is a stick-up."

"Well, like he says — a lot of people get hurt that don't deserve it."

"They sure worried about you, those poor innocents," Reeves said. "But, hell — you go on ahead with your new scheme. Take on the law in his own backyard."

"Would you go along?"

Reeves laughed. "Not today, Frank. Not tomorrow, neither. I came along for something that made a whole lot of sense — like the Salvation bank. But you want to play games, you go right ahead." He said it all with a curled lip, and his eyes fastened rigidly on Booth's face. Booth turned to Buchanan.

"Luth is right," he said. "Just playing games. We came for money — a bankful of it."

"And when you take it — what've you got then, Booth?" Buchanan asked him.

"The only thing in this life that counts, that's what I've got."

"Even if you lose the likes of the girl you married?"

Ellen had been listening to it all, from the hallway, and now she came into the room.

"Thank you," she said quietly to Buchanan. "I know how much it means to you to be gone from here — how much you were willing to give up." She turned around and faced her husband squarely. "This man owes you nothing," she told him. "Not a *damn* thing," she added for emphasis. "But he offered you — us — a chance to make a go of our marriage. You turned it down, Frank. What you did was choose a life with this rapist and thief for a life with me. And I'm leaving you."

"To go with him?" Booth asked.

"To *travel* with him," she said. "To ride along under his protection!"

Reeves guffawed. "That's a new word for it," he said and Buchanan hit him right in his offending mouth. The effort was costly, so far as his own shoulder was concerned, but there was full compensation in seeing Luther slam back against the wall, bounce from it and then sink floorward with a glassy-eyed expression on his slack face.

"Now you see what I meant," Ellen Booth said to her husband and promptly walked out of the kitchen. Buchanan hung back, troubled by the new development.

"Go on after her, Booth," he urged the other man. "Take her down by that little pool and talk things out. By the time you get back I'll have this Reeves bum gone and forgotten . . ."

Booth shook his head. "There's nothing to talk out. I'm getting even with Hallett and Luth is my partner."

"So be it," Buchanan said, giving up on him, turning away.

Some twenty minutes later Buchanan swung into his saddle, began walking his horse in tight circles to test the hoof. She seemed relaxed under him, even a little too relaxed, and he felt she would make it to journey's end without discomfort.

Wish I could say the same for myself, the man thought unhappily, seeing Ellen and Juanita emerge from the house and start toward the horse they were going to share for the trip. It was not that he could find it in himself to say that Ellen's decision was a wrong one. After waiting

165

for her man as she had, Booth was sure letting her down now. Buchanan knew he was guessing, but he imagined that having this ranch to come back to had been the one bright spot in the girl's hopes for the future. There'd be no coming back to it with Frank Booth now — not after he robbed the bank in Salvation. They'd be on the dodge from then on — running, running, always looking back over their shoulders.

No, there was no blaming her for pulling stakes. What Buchanan didn't like was his role in the break-up. It couldn't be helped, he supposed, but he sure wished that Frank Booth would come to his senses.

He dismounted, hoisted Juanita into the saddle of Bull Hynman's horse, then stood for a moment beside Ellen.

"You sure you want to go?" he asked.

She nodded her head.

"Did you talk to him at all?"

"We said good-by," Ellen said, her voice catching in her throat.

"Look," Buchanan said. "How about me going inside and booting Luther on out of here? Frank wouldn't try that job alone . . ."

"No," she said. "That wouldn't change anything. Frank would have to break with Reeves on his own decision."

"Yeh, I guess," Buchanan admitted gloomily.

"Let's get started," Ellen said. "Would you give me a hand up?"

Buchanan started to and Frank Booth's voice

cracked out at him from the house.

"Touch my wife and you're a dead man!"

Buchanan looked around. Booth was kneeling before a bedroom window, aiming a rifle over the ledge. The door opened and Luther Reeves stepped through, also armed with a rifle. There was a look of impatience about Reeves, as though he were being restrained from doing something he wanted very much to do.

"Go on, back away from her!" Booth commanded, motioning with the rifle barrel. "Ride out with your Mex — and keep riding."

Reeves was the one who had all of Buchanan's attention, and he very slowly edged himself between the man and Ellen.

"I said get away from her!" Booth shouted wildly.

Without turning his head, Buchanan began speaking very calmly to Ellen.

"When I count to three," he said, "throw yourself flat on the ground. One —"

"What are you going to do?" Ellen demanded.

"Take Reeves," he said, "One, two —"

"No!" Ellen cried, and then she was out from behind Buchanan, moving away swiftly. She stopped and turned to him, began shaking her head emotionally. "You wouldn't have a chance," she said. "Not a chance. Do what they want, Buchanan. Ride away from here."

Buchanan couldn't risk a glance at her. He and Reeves were staring into each other's eyes.

"Go on," Reeves said goadingly. "Go for it."

"Let him leave, Luth," Frank Booth said from the window.

"He don't want to, Frank. He wants to show me his draw. Go ahead, you sonofabitch — show me . . ."

Ellen stepped directly in their line of fire, her slim back to Reeves. "I've changed my mind," she said to Buchanan. "I want to stay here. *I really want to stay here.* Even — even if you won I'd stay."

Some expression softened the lines of Buchanan's face then, some of the warmth crept back into his eyes.

"Reeves," he called.

"Yeah?"

"Why don't you give these two people a break? Why don't you pull out and let them work things out different?"

"Why don't you mind your goddam business?" came the surly answer to the proposition. "Why don't you fish for that shooter and stop crawlin'?"

"Go now," Ellen said. "Please go away!"

"All right." He backed off toward the waiting mustang, not able to trust the man with the rifle even that far. And when he mounted he kept his right hand free, only inches from the .45. But Booth, apparently, had gotten some sort of promise out of Reeves. Not to shoot without provocation, maybe. Still he watched him like a hawk as he moved up alongside Juanita.

"*Vamos,*" he told the girl.

They started off at a walk, and then Buchanan

168

chanced a farewell glance at Ellen Booth.

"So long," he called back to her with a touch of his hand to the brim of his hat. "Wish you all the luck you deserve."

She waved her own hand, but for some reason said nothing. He looked at her again, more closely — and now he saw the tears streaming down her cheeks. He reined up.

"No!" Ellen cried. "No! I want you to go away!"

Buchanan kneed his horse, impatiently, and rode away from there at a gallop.

Chapter Twelve

It had been so long since Sid Hallett had taken a licking from anyone that two days after the event he was still brooding about the upset Buchanan had handed him. (Which would have surprised the tall man, who didn't mark his brief sojourn in Salvation as a personal triumph when he had picked up two new bullet scars, assorted maulings and had to be rescued from the field of battle by a pair of women. Buchanan, when he ever got around to writing his memoirs, would briefly mention the clash with Hallett & Co. as a Mexican stand-off — one in which everybody takes some amount of clobbering and no issue is decided.)

But the High Sheriff and Good Shepherd of Salvation considered that the arrival and the departure of the transient rider had cost him a great deal of personal prestige and standing in his town. The death of Lafe Jenkins was an affront, a reflection on the efficiency of his office — especially since Pete Nabor and some other loudmouths claimed that the deputy had his man in his sights and even fired three times. The Bull Hynman incident could be shushed up. No one need know that an unarmed man had not only overpowered the mighty Bull and laid him cold, but had added insult to injury by locking the chief deputy in a cell with his own key. But Sid Hallett knew it had happened and the thing rankled in his mind, chipped away at the belief he'd grown to have in his invincibility.

The sheriff had gone through the proper motions, of course. He still showed an outward appearance of stern, cold dignity and he had clamped the lid down tight on Salvation. The curfew was moved up an hour, and now Hynman and Enos enforced it along River Street. Doc Allen had been promptly arrested and jailed for aiding and abetting a fugitive. Birdy Warren's saloon was padlocked, and even Maude had been told to suspend operations until Hallett was sure that the town was obediently at heel again, that the example of Buchanan didn't give anyone else ideas about challenging the vested authority here.

But left alone the man brooded, let his mind roam all-unbridled over the past, and for the first time in his career the man began to see the events and the people in their proper focus.

His thoughts, for instance, ranged as far back as the city of Boston, where he had been born. Brought into the world by a midwife who couldn't save his mother, handed over to a proud, cynical maternal grandmother whose own father had helped condemn witches to the torch in nearby Salem. Hallett was also the maternal name, Sidney's father being an unidentified sailor. All the time that he lived with Grandmother Hallett the bitter old woman never let him forget that he had been begotten in sin.

This, however, didn't prevent him from entering the Harvard School of Divinity after earning his BA at the University, but might have had something to do with shocking the churchmen's college into dismissing him in the midst of his second semester. (There was an essay involved — according to young Sidney's explanation to his grandmother — one that questioned the legal status of Mary and Joseph when Jesus was born. Hallett's conclusion was that their child had been born out of wedlock, and that all such children are touched with divinity. The Dean denied that this wildly written paper had anything to do with his separation. He told the grandmother, in person, that her ward had been found publicly drunk in Copley Square by the prefect, and at the time in the company of a woman well-known to the police of Boston as a harlot.)

The grandmother passed away a year later, rather conveniently, and Sidney fell heir to a tidy twenty-thousand dollars. He fled Boston immediately, headed west, a young man too thin for his extreme height, too much given to weird, unorthodox interpretations of the Bible — and too easily tempted by women. In Chicago he was jailed for enticing a female under the legal age of consent. He jumped the two-hundred dollar bail and made his way to Dodge. There was no law against enticing in that wide-open town, not even a God — but even so, Sidney Hallett was given eight hours notice to leave town by the U.S. Marshal.

He made several stopovers on his continuing journey west, most of them of short duration, but he eventually gravitated to the melting pot that was San Francisco. By now he had become very cautious about violating the law, and grievously envious of the men who enforced the law. Side by side with that ambition grew an ever increasing fanaticism with religion.

Sidney was, by nature, a tight man with a dollar. But some of the things he had to have cost money, and the twenty thousand began to dwindle. It was when he had five-thousand dollars left that he 'discovered' the old Mexican tract which he bought from the new State of California and re-named Salvation.

Salvation was an idea he had been nurturing in his secret mind for some time. It was a town that he would run, in every respect, and anyone who wanted to settle there would be beholden to Sidney Hallett. He owned the land, five square miles of it, and instead of selling sites he leased them for a term of ninety-nine years. And each lease contained any number of 'moral turpitude' clauses which allowed the landlord to cancel the contract for nearly any reason at all. No wonder, then, that the merchants paid strict attention to whatever Hallett decreed — whether he spoke from the pulpit or wrote his own laws in the sheriff's office. No wonder that the Selectmen automatically reelected him as peace officer, that the Deacons renewed his appointment as pastor.

For over a decade now he had run things his way, directed peoples' very existence. Until last Sunday. A lone drifter had shown his organization to be soft, vulnerable, and the experience left Sid Hallett shaken in his self-confidence, indecisive.

Right after Lafe had been shot, for example. Should he send his men after the wounded Buchanan and the two females — or should he keep them here? Hynman wanted to give chase, violently, but Hallett worried that Hynman might be killed himself — and Enos. Then he would have no guns left at all, and no time to import others if he had guessed right that Frank Booth and Luther Reeves were already enroute.

So he had kept his guns close by, for protection, and that in itself was an admission of insecurity. Now, on this everlastingly hot, bright Tuesday afternoon, the man sat behind his desk deep in thought, meditating about the past, speculating about the future, and from no particular source he got the inspiration for next Sunday's sermon.

It would be the return of the prodigal — except that his version would differ radically from the scripture. For Frank Booth would play the prodigal. As Hallett outlined his thoughts he knew he could fall back on the Old Testament for some unyielding, show-the-sinner-no-mercy quotations that would give his sermon the mantle of 'truth.'

Booth would now be akin to a leper. Association would mean contamination. He should, therefore, be struck down on sight, destroyed. It would require some obtuse language, some dramatics from the pulpit, but Hallett felt confident that when he was done the town would be with him.

As he began to write out his sermon the door of the office opened and Bull Hynman entered. Hynman looked older, somehow — looked haggard and worn out. The long hours on duty were getting him down, the constant patrolling in the merciless sun, and on top of the unexpected work load he had to live with his dark thoughts about Buchanan. His mind was murderous on that sore subject — as sore as the welt at the base of his skull — and the knowledge that he would never get another crack at Buchanan only heaped fresh coal on his sullen anger, left him badly frustrated. Yesterday morning, for instance, he had stood above Lafe Jenkins' open grave and amazed everyone at the funeral with the depth and obvious genuineness of his grief. He had even been seen to brush a hairy hand across his eyes. Hynman did feel sorry, and it had been a tear, but only because the pine box being lowered into the earth didn't contain the body of Buchanan.

Lafe Jenkins? Hell, that scudder had been gettin' too big for his britches for over a year now.

"Where is Enos?" Hallett asked him now, looking up from his writing.

"Don't know."

"*Don't know?* By God, you'd better know!"

"He's down to River Street," Hynman said, his own voice peevish. "That's where he's supposed to be."

Hallett glared at him. "Maybe your responsibilities are getting too much for you," he said coldly. "You may not be as helpful to me as you used to be."

"Ah, it's this heat," Hynman said. "And lookin' for ghosts, mornin', noon and night."

"What do you mean, looking for ghosts?"

"Booth and Reeves. Sid, they ain't comin' back here."

"And I say that they are. I also say —"

What Hallett also would say Hynman was not to know, for at that moment a cry went up at Sinai Street, a voice shouting bad news for Salvation:

"THE BANK'S BEEN ROBBED! SHERIFF — THEY ROBBED THE BANK!"

They had for a fact — and after two long years of thinking about it, of planning it, of living with it, the thing had gone off so ridiculously easy that Frank Booth almost felt let down. Not his partner, though. The easier things came the better it suited Luther Reeves — especially the sometimes risky chore of holding up banks.

They had talked it over one more time following Buchanan's departure from the ranch. Reeves had liked the news that the law in Salvation was shy

176

one deputy, and he liked the weather, the heat that would keep people off the streets, make the town itself indolent and lazy. It was Reeves' suggestion that they hit the bank at two o'clock, siesta time, and shortly after noon they started down from the hills, watched from her bedroom by Ellen — who had hoped right up until that last minute that Frank would change his mind.

It never occurred to him. He was committed irrevocably to having his revenge on Sid Hallett, on Cyrus Martin, on anyone and everyone who had been responsible for his going to prison.

They came into Salvation from the south, along Genesis Street, and as Booth saw one familiar landmark after another he felt a giddiness go through him, as if it were unreal that he was returning. But that passed, passed at the intersection at Sinai, when he found himself staring at the squat little building marked BANK OF SALVATION. It seemed even smaller than he remembered.

"This is it," Reeves said. "Let's go."

They went. Directly across Sinai, walking their horses, trying to look as much like two punchers as possible. They dismounted, tied their animals loosely to the rail, and sauntered inside.

And for once, Pete Nabor missed something that was happening in Salvation. The old man dozed in his rocker while his life savings were being stolen across the street.

Reeves walked directly to the single teller's cage, stuck the long barrel of his .44 into the cashier's frightened face.

"Put it all in a sack," Reeves told him. "Don't hold a dollar out or I'll blow your head clean off your shoulders!"

Frank Booth's destination was Martin's private office. The bank president looked up from his desk, annoyed at the intrusion, and then his mouth dropped open and his body began shaking uncontrollably.

"It's me, Martin. Frank Booth. Swing that safe open inside thirty seconds or I'll kill you."

"No," the old man said. "Don't shoot me. Don't . . ."

"Get to work on the safe then."

Martin did, but his hands shook so that he bungled the combination that he could have dialed in his sleep. The second time the tumblers fell into place and the door opened.

"Stand aside," Booth ordered. He knelt before the safe, began filling sacks with the thousands of dollars resting in there. There was also a money box, locked. "Give me the key to this," he ordered.

"It's at home," Martin said. "I swear to you that it's home."

Booth dropped the box into the sack, and when he hoisted it to his shoulder he had a sizable weight to carry.

"Stay right here," he told the banker, backing out of the office. Reeves was waiting for him.

"Got it all?"

"Everything."

"They don't keep it anywheres else?"

"No."

"Come on then."

They left the bank, got back on their horses and rode on out Genesis again. That's all there was to it.

Except for the part of the job that Frank Booth didn't know about. He learned, though, an hour and a half later, just as their horses were topping the last steep rise before coming onto the ranch.

"Hold up a minute, Frank," Luther told him from behind. Booth reined in, looked around questioningly.

"What's the matter, Luth? What're you holding that rifle on me for?"

"Get down off your horse, Frank."

"Down? Why? What're you going to do?"

"Gonna kill you, old buddy," Reeves told him and actually sounded regretful. "Got to," he added.

"*Got to?*" Booth repeated, his voice cracking, his face stunned. "We're partners, Luth! Share and share alike . . ."

"Frank, it ain't *just* the money. My problem with you is, you're not cut out for this work. Why you almost backed out on me this very mornin' . . ."

"But I didn't, though! I went through with it, didn't I?"

"It ain't in your blood, son. I couldn't depend on you. Now climb down off that horse. I don't want her all spooked-up." His tone was suddenly curt, businesslike.

Booth laid both hands over his saddlehorn, spoke earnestly.

"You couldn't do it, Luth," he said to the other man. "You *know* you couldn't shoot me. Not the pals we been . . ."

"It was gonna be sooner or later," Reeves told him flatly. "Now it's got to be sooner. Get off that horse."

"Why?" Booth shouted, though there wasn't six feet between them. "Why has it *got* to be now?"

"On account of that pretty blonde wife of yours," Reeves answered. "Her and me don't want you underfoot, do we?"

Booth's eyes flared in anger — but only for one brief, flickering moment. In the next instant his glance had dropped from Reeves' face to the long barrel of the rifle and it was then that he forfeited his manhood.

"I won't, Luth," he said, shaking his head for emphasis. "I won't be in your way at all. Look. We'll split the money right here and now. I'll take my half and head south with it. I'll keep going till I'm across the border. *All right, Luth?*" The words had spewed from his mouth in a torrent, and when he was through there was a long silence.

"Get off the horse," Reeves told him. "I'm runnin' a little short on time —"

Booth spread his heels, raked the horse's belly

with his spurs and sent it plunging headlong toward the top of the hill. Reeves set the rifle stock
against his armpit, sighted along the barrel and
fired at the desperately retreating figure.

Chapter Thirteen

They had ridden off at noon, and for a long while afterward Ellen Booth had stayed at the bedroom window, gazing moodily out at the land, her spirit numbed, her mind locked in a vise. She felt trapped — trapped by the very surroundings that had once been such a happy and carefree home. And just as those days were gone beyond recall, so she felt about the future, that it was lost, that her life was ended. It was a foreboding the girl couldn't shake, a certainty that there was an act of violence in the making from which she would not escape.

After a time she stirred from the window, began wandering aimlessly through the house she knew and loved so dearly. She had been born within these walls, lived here for eighteen wonderful years, been married in this very parlor — and now in her melancholy thoughts she was saying good-by.

It was the same despondency that led her out of the house, guided her steps to the secluded little spring that was such a rich storehouse of memories. What a part this place had played in the life of Ellen Henry.

'Ellen Henry.' Not once in over three years had she thought of herself as anyone but Ellen

Booth, Mrs. Frank Booth, and as she gazed at her reflection in the bright green water it seemed very important to know whether she had used her maiden name because there was no connection between Mrs. Frank Booth and the pond, or whether her subconscious mind no longer considered her married.

There was no clear answer to the question, and the longer she stared into the shimmering water the less it seemed to matter. The less anything mattered. She had a sudden urge then to be in the pool, to be comforted by it, and in a matter of moments she had stepped out of her brief clothing and dove beneath the cool surface.

If time could only be stopped, she thought as she floated around in the water. If she could just stay here forever . . .

The gunfire sounded very clear and sharp in the still air. She counted three shots, evenly spaced, and then a formidable silence. Quickly, almost feverishly, Ellen regained the bank and dressed herself again. But she had no intention of investigating the shots. Instead, she huddled down right here, and it was as if some sixth sense told her that whoever had fired the gun would be looking for her.

The first slug from the rifle plowed into the money pouch. The second and third lifted Frank Booth clear out of the saddle, but his right boot got wedged in the stirrup and the frightened horse dragged him head down over the rough ground for another fifty feet before Luther Reeves could halt the animal.

Reeves dismounted, freed the caught foot and let the dead man lie where he was while he recovered the nearby pouch and led both horses on foot the rest of the way to the house.

Reeves hadn't wanted to make such a racket — just a single bullet between Booth's eyes and then take the woman by surprise. But he guessed that she had heard the noise, and when a search of the house didn't produce her he told himself that that was all right, too. Hunting game came natural to the man, and as he started out to flush her from her hiding place he felt excited, expectant.

And as part of the sport he left the most obvious spot to last — the thick, hedgelike growth of foliage off to the left. His sharp eyes marked the trail of matted grass leading up to it, picked out the exact point where someone had parted the brush.

He peered through, looked into the shaded glen. But Reeves was no lover of nature and the place had no appeal for him. He preferred the house.

"I've found ya, sweetheart," he called out in a voice that he thought was cajoling. "Come on out and say hello to your big new man."

Ellen hugged the side of the bank in terror.

"Don't be unfriendly now, little darlin'. Just come on out of there."

He scowled when she still kept silent. There was a lot of money lying around loose back at the house and he wanted to get back to it.

"Was I you, sweetheart, I wouldn't make old Luther mad at me," he said then, warningly. "Luther wants to treat you like a real gent, so don't you go spoilin' the fun."

Ellen thought that if she didn't stop hearing his voice she would scream. She had begun to work her way along the bank toward the opposite side, knowing all the while how futile it was, that she was only postponing the inevitable. For this little space was now her whole world, and in that world were just two people — herself and a man named Luther Reeves.

"All *right!*" she heard him shout from above. "That's the way you want it to happen, that's the way you'll get it!" He broke through the foliage, and his heavy footfalls pounded nearer and nearer.

Suddenly it was very still, and the girl raised her head slowly. He stood looking down at her — legs spread wide, hands on hips — leering down at her, and she knew that there couldn't be a crueler sight than the one he presented.

"Do I got to come fetch ya, honey?" Reeves asked insolently.

Ellen shook her head, said "No" in a voice that was barely audible.

"Then move, damn it! Get yourself on up here, woman!"

She started to mount the incline on legs that had lost the sensation of feeling, lost her footing briefly near the top, and when he reached out to take her hand she recoiled with an expression of loathing. He grabbed her then, roughly, pulled her up over the ledge and hard against him. She struggled to twist away, to avert her face, but an arm encircled her waist, a hand was in her damp hair, forcing her head back, and his mouth fastened itself on hers with a lusting, half-crazed hunger.

He broke the embrace just as savagely, held her at arms length. She stared into his face, saw herself stripped naked in the eyes that devoured her.

"The house," he said hoarsely. "Get to the house quick." She tried again to break free. He swung her in front of him, pushed her to the opening in the brush and on out into the open. She stumbled, fell to her knees, only to be pulled to her feet again, dragged along irresistibly.

Toward the house, toward *home* — and in the midst of all her fearfulness Ellen knew one moment of pure and terrible clarity. Let him take her right here, let her remember this nightmare as happening in this field that was like any other field. But not in the house, not *home*.

She had fallen down again, been jerked erect again, but that was not what had broken her chain of thoughts. Nor could she tell if he had seen it, too — the horse and rider, still small figures in the distance, not possible to recognize.

But you don't always have to see something with your eyes. Your heart tells you. Ellen's heart told her that it was Buchanan.

All at once, and to the vast surprise of Luther Reeves, she began laughing. Great peals of laughter, joyous, unrestrained, and to look at her was even more puzzling, for she was crying at the same time.

Reeves' reaction to that — as to everything he didn't understand — was brute force. He doubled Ellen's arm behind her back, shoved her ahead of him more violently — then let loose of her altogether when he spotted the oncoming horseman for himself.

His saddle and rifle rested atop the corral fence, and as Reeves broke in that direction Ellen made a dash for the house. Once inside she climbed immediately into the attic, went to the locker and found the small-caliber hunting pistol that had been a birthday present half-a-dozen years before. She loaded it, and even as she was descending to the floor below the sound of firing commenced in the yard.

She ran through the house to her own room, closed the door and sat down on the edge of the bed. There, with the pistol held tensely in her lap, she waited, listening to the duel being waged outside the window, distinguishing between the sure, steady crack of the powerful rifle, the less-authoritative sound of the handgun.

Then, with a suddenness that was ominous, there was quiet. A minute passed. Another. Her straining ears heard the front door open and close, listened to a man's bootheels coming down hard on the bare floor of the hallway. Ellen cocked the pistol, raised it from her lap and aimed it inward, directly below her wildly heaving breast.

The doorknob turned and the door swung open.

"Everything's all right now," Buchanan said and that was too much for Ellen. With a soft sighing sound the girl fell over on the bed in a faint.

The actual fainting spell lasted only a minute or two, but Ellen passed from that into a sleep of exhaustion. When she did awake again it was quite dark in the bedroom, and for a while she had the queer feeling of not being able to remember what had happened or even why she was here. Then she did remember, and the girl got out of the bed quickly, left the room and walked through the empty, unlighted house.

"Buchanan?" she called out uncertainly. No one answered. She brought a match then from the kitchen, got the parlor lamp glowing, and was astonished a moment later to find herself in the presence of a great deal of money — all of it the property of the bank down in Salvation. There were two gunnysacks, crammed nearly to overflowing, and Ellen was staring at them in a very disquieted manner when she heard a loose board on the porch groan under a heavy weight. The front door opened.

"Buchanan?" she called again, this time in fear.

"Right," came the sound of his voice, and then the man himself appeared in the parlor entrance. The sight of him standing there, dwarfing all else around him, released a flood of memories in the girl's mind — their sum and total being a feeling of reassurance.

"I thought you'd gone off again," she said, trying to speak normally, to put a checkrein on the unnormal emotions that were coming so close to the surface.

Buchanan was studying her as well, marking what the lamplight did to the planes of her fine face, how it complimented the warm gold coloring of her hair. He looked very unhappy.

"Do you know about your husband?" he asked.

"I think so," Ellen said. "Reeves killed him?"

Buchanan nodded. "I buried them kind of close together," he told her, a note of apology in his voice. "But I marked where he is in case you want to have him moved somewheres better."

"Thank you," she said.

"You're welcome."

"What made you — I mean, how did you happen to come back?"

"Damned if I — beg your pardon. Couldn't explain, exactly," he amended. "Guess I just put myself in Luther's boots. Kind of a troublemaker, that one."

Ellen smiled. "Kind of," she agreed. "Where's Juanita?"

That gave Buchanan something to smile about. "On her way home," he said. "Finally. Met the stage out of Sacramento up the trail a ways. Bound down to Monterey — with no mail stop in Salvation."

189

"Tell me — was she happy to get aboard?" Ellen asked. At the question Buchanan looked down at her suspiciously, made a tell-tale gesture of rubbing his jaw with the palm of his hand.

"She was happy enough," he said, recalling the objections the girl had raised before accepting the fact that they couldn't travel together indefinitely. Then, changing the subject, he jerked a thumb toward the sacks of money.

"Thought I'd haul that plunder back to town," he said.

"When?"

"Now. Might help a few folks get a night's rest — knowing they're not cleaned out."

"But it won't be safe for you in Salvation."

"I didn't figure on holding a parade or anything," he told her drily. "Just ride up to the banker's back porch and drop it off."

Ellen nodded. "I guess you could do that. Mr. Martin lives outside town." She paused for a moment, looking at him. "Can I come along?" she asked.

"I was going to suggest it," Buchanan said. "This wouldn't be much of a place to stay tonight."

"Not alone," she said, her eyes full on his face.

"No," he answered quietly. "Not alone. Well, I'll get the loot in the saddlebags and then we can be off." He picked up both sacks and went out with them. When she was alone Ellen asked herself pointblank if she felt ashamed about impulsively inviting him to spend the night with her. The answer was *no*. She felt regret and perhaps a sense of relief that her heart had expressed itself — that the struggle against her own conscience was over.

Buchanan strode back into the room, carrying a metal box in his hand. She saw immediately that something had made him angry.

"Maybe we ought to have that parade after all," he said.

"Why, what is it?"

He set the box on the table beneath the lamp, pulled the lid open. "Somewhere along the line a bullet busted the lock on this thing," he told her. "Take a look at what dropped out when I went to put it in the saddlebag."

Ellen looked inside the box. There was no money there, only various documents. One was a mortgage held by Cyrus Martin personally, one a promissory note, one a will — and at the bottom, where Buchanan had replaced it, an envelope bearing a curious message in a careful script.

To whom it may concern, it read, *in the event of my death by foul play.*

"Take out the note inside," Buchanan told Ellen.

She slid the folded paper from the envelope, began reading it in silence. As each sentence passed beneath the girl's eyes her face became more stricken. She turned, finally, to Buchanan. "Can this be true?" she asked in a strained voice. "Could that terrible man possibly have done such a thing?"

"Be important to you to find out, wouldn't it?" Buchanan asked, taking the letter from her fingers and replacing it in the envelope.

"Yes," Ellen answered. "Yes, it would be very important. But what chance would Hallett ever give you?"

"Let's ride down into that Bible-spouter's town and find out," Buchanan said.

Chapter Fourteen

At the first clamorous peal of the church bell, Sidney Hallett came to his feet with an angry, startled expression.

"What's that?" he demanded of the equally surprised Bull Hynman. "Who gave orders to ring the bell?"

"Not me," Hynman said. "The posse ain't due to ride till before daybreak."

The bell kept up its strident, insistent sound, beckoning all within its hearing to gather round.

"By God," Hallett said, "some one had better not be changing my orders! Come with me!" His orders were for an armed group to head for Booth's ranch and reach it at the time when they would least be expected. Enos, meanwhile, had been dispatched north to alert the law in that direction. Another man was doing the same to the south.

"What's up, Sheriff? They catch the crooks?" Hallett was asked now as he made the turn into Genesis Street. He gave the man no answer, observed the heavy turnout of people hurrying as he was to the church. *Someone,* he promised grimly, *would pay for this.* Enough had gone wrong already, and the man's unruly temper was at a dangerous point.

And still the bell tolled, as if deliberately goading him to some act of violence.

"Go up in the tower," he told Hynman furiously, "and haul that damn fool down here by the scruff of the neck!"

Hynman hurried on ahead to obey, shouldering the men and women of Salvation aside as he went. *Jesus,* he thought, *I never knew how loud that bell was.* It never occurred to him to wonder what size man it would take to produce such a prodigious loudness. It still didn't as he mounted the steep flight of stairs to the belfry, climbed closer to the marvelous din. Then he was standing in the tower itself, staring at the two silhouetted forms in the place with him. One was unmistakably Ellen Booth. There could be no doubt of it. And the other, both hands engaged with the bell-rope . . . !

Bull Hynman knew he had him. Had him with an easy draw, a straight shot — but he didn't have Ellen, whose warning scream went unheard, who shoved Buchanan with all her might. Hynman's gunblast shattered the darkness and the bullet found some scant opening between the bodies of the man and girl across the way. Rattled, he fired again. Buchanan's gun came up. The first slug doubled Hynman in two. The second and third drove all life out of him.

"*Ellen!*" Buchanan said hoarsely, bending to the girl who lay face down on the flooring. "Are you all right?"

"Yes," she said. "Yes. Are you?"

"I think so," he told her. "You sure are some handy in a pinch."

"You're some handy yourself, mister."

"Some stupid," he said, "not to have an eye out for company. Didn't expect to get such a fast response out of them." He lifted the girl to her feet.

"HYNMAN!" Hallett shouted from down below. "What's going on up there?"

"You're yelling in the wrong direction, Sheriff, if you want your deputy," Buchanan called back.

"You!"

"Me, and I'm coming down. Stand clear."

Buchanan started the descent unhesitatingly, Ellen close behind, shielded by his body. At the foot of the steps Hallett was paying strict attention to the unwavering gun in Buchanan's big hand. Now he started to back away from it, into the circle of people gathered in the church foyer.

Then Buchanan was standing before them all.

"Glad to see such a nice turnout, folks," he told them. "If you'll go inside and make yourselves comfortable there's something I think you ought to hear."

"Hold on!" Sid Hallett said, stepping forward, turning his back to Buchanan and speaking with his familiar authority. "Return to your homes," he told the sizable assemblage. "This man is a killer and worse. He'll not give orders while I'm still the law in Salvation."

A hand came down irreverently on his shoulder, turning him around.

"That's one of the subjects on the agenda, Sheriff," Buchanan informed him. "Lead the way inside."

Hallett looked up into the other man's face as if he might defy the flat command. Then, with an angry grimace, he pushed Buchanan's hand from his shoulder and walked on inside the church proper with the air of someone still very much in command. His steps carried him to the pulpit, and he mounted it familiarly. Buchanan walked with Ellen to the other side, stood on the same spot that Juanita had during the farcical trial two nights before. He raised his long arm for quiet.

"This won't take long," he said. "First off, is Cyrus Martin among the present?"

"Yes," a voice answered and the banker stood up in his regular pew. "What do you want of me?"

"Mrs. Booth found some money that belongs to your bank."

"What?" Martin asked, raising his voice above the instant murmuring. "You have the stolen funds?"

"A gent named Pete Nabor is keeping an eye on them over at the rooming house."

A happy cry went up from the spectators. Buchanan asked for silence again. Then, from his shirtfront, he took the envelope.

"Mr. Martin," he said, "three years ago you wrote a letter. I'd like you to stand up in that pulpit alongside the sheriff and read it to these folks."

"A letter . . . ?"

"It was in the strongbox that was taken from the bank today. If you don't want to read it, I will."

Martin looked dazed, stood there shaking his head from side to side. Buchanan crossed over to the pulpit.

"Stand down, preacher man," he told Hallett. "There's a sinner wants to get something off his chest."

Hallett looked down at Buchanan, then over to Cyrus Martin, his face wary.

"Stand down or I'll pull you out of that pulpit," Buchanan said. Hallett climbed down and Buchanan replaced him.

"This is a letter, folks," he announced to the crowd. "It's written 'to whom it may concern' — and I think it concerns everybody here, myself included." He unfolded the note and began reading:

" 'I live in constant fear of injury and even death at the hands of Sidney A. Hallett, the High Sheriff of Salvation. For that reason I am writing this document as a last means of defense against Hallett. If it fails in that, at least I will have had some measure of retribution from the grave.' "

Buchanan looked up briefly. "You sure you don't want to read this yourself, Martin?" he asked. The banker, staring at Hallett, shook his head. Buchanan began again.

" 'Three months ago,' " the letter continued,

" 'a young teller in the Salvation Bank was convicted of embezzling five thousand dollars of the bank's funds. His name is Frank Booth and of that crime he is completely innocent —' "

The stirring among the audience caused him to pause.

" 'Completely innocent,' " he repeated when it was quiet once more. " 'There was no embezzlement and no money is unaccounted for. Frank Booth's ring, which was used as damaging evidence against him, was appropriated by me when Booth laid it aside in the washroom. A man identified as a U.S. Marshal was actually a former prisoner employed by Sidney Hallett for the trial and paid another sum to return east. There is no such woman living in San Francisco named Ruby Fowler. She was created by Sidney Hallett . . .' "

That was as far as Buchanan got. Two shots exploded over his voice. The first, fired from a Derringer pistol, struck Cyrus Martin in the chest. The second, fired into his own brain, killed Sidney Hallett.

The throng crowded around the bodies — curious, shocked, angry, above all, disillusioned. Buchanan came down from the pulpit and slipped out of the church unnoticed.

Except for Ellen, who caught up with him in the street.

"You're leaving alone?" she asked.

"You got no reason not to stay here now," he said.

"No, I can live here now," she agreed. "But if you asked me, I'd go with you."

"I'm not your style, Ellen. Too rootless."

"You're that," she admitted in her frank way. "But you'll also sink roots someday."

"Someday. Not tomorrow, though. Going to work for the railroad tomorrow."

Ellen held out her slim hand and he took it in his.

"I'm not even going to say thank you again, Buchanan. Just good-by."

"Good-by to you, Ellen. It's been a pleasure to know a real lady."

She smiled at that, enigmatically, and as he rode off down Genesis Street he was left to wonder if he had said the right thing to her or not. Then he was abreast of the hotel and Pete Nabor hailed him from his all-but-permanent station.

"Get the job done, big fella?"

"Well, the job of sheriff is open. Interested?"

"Hell no! But why don't you stay around and keep the peace?"

Buchanan laughed. "Keep the peace? Me? Old man, I can't even keep a date in Sacramento."

"That where you bound?"

"Yessir. And I'm going to get there if I have to tote this horse on *my* back. See you, Pete!"

"*Hasta luego!*" Nabor shouted after him.

William R. Cox was born in Peapack, New Jersey. His early career was in newspaper journalism. In the late 1930s he began writing sports, crime, and adventure stories for the magazine market, and he made his debut as a Western writer with "Night of the Blood Bucket Raid" in *Dime Western* in the January, 1941 issue. It is worth noting that his Western story debut was with the first of several stories to feature a series character, Terry Glenn. During the 1940s Cox created a number of other series characters for the magazine market, most notably the Whistler Kid who appeared regularly in *10 Story Western* and Duke Bagley whose adventures usually were featured in *Star Western*. "The short story form was blissful until there were no markets," he once recalled. In the 1950s and 1960s Cox turned to television and wrote at least a hundred teleplays for such series as "Broken Arrow," "Dick Powell's Zane Grey Theatre," "The Virginian," and "Bonanza." He also won a host of readers writing original paperback Western novels, the best known of which are novels about the adventures of two series characters originally published by Fawcett Gold Medal: Cemetery Jones in a series published under his own byline and the Tom Buchanan series which appeared under the house name, Jonas Ward. Dale L. Walker in the second edition of TWENTIETH CENTURY WESTERN WRITERS commented that William R. Cox's Western "novels are noted for their 'pageturner' pace, realistic dialogue, and frequent Colt-and-Winchester gun play. The series of novels built around the strong West Texas character, Tom Buchanan, are very typical Cox Westerns."